The Axel Files:

Florence's Floozy

By Jerry Bader

Who Will Find The Savola Diamond,
And Who Will Die Trying?

Copyright © 2022 Jerry Bader

ISBN Paperback: 978-1-988647-79-1

Hard Cover: 978-1-988647-80-7

Ebook: 978-1-988647-78-4

Chapter 1
Dace's Doll

Hotel Geneve, Mexico City, 1941

Otto Dace enters the café in the lobby of the Hotel Geneve. His seven-year-old son, Heinz Victor, and his five-year-old daughter, Florence Katrina, cling to him. The little girl is uneasy. She grips her father's hand as tight as she can. The trip from Zurich to Buenos Aires to Mexico City was long, scary, and uncomfortable. The children longed to return to their home in Switzerland, but that wasn't an option.

Otto finds seats in the lobby café. He tries to comfort the children by ordering American-style ice cream sodas: butterscotch for Heinz and chocolate for Florence. But no amount of ice cream can calm Otto's nerves. He isn't used to the anxiety: not because of the war; not because of his wife's recent passing; and not because he fled his superficially neutral homeland. What makes Otto Dace nervous is the extraordinary pink gemstone sewn into the lining of his trench coat. He doesn't dare take-off the overcoat despite the obsessive summer heat.

The *Nebel des Krieges* created the opportunity to escape Europe with the *Conte's* prized possession. Only time will tell if he'll get away with this *vertrauensbruch*. He felt bad about betraying the *Conte*, but the war changed everything. *Es ist jeder für sich*: it's everyone for themselves. Who knew if the *Conte* would even survive the conflict. Otto had his own priorities and an obligation to his children. He had to secure their future.

Otto waits for his contact while Heinz and Florence try to enjoy their ice cream treats. He is supposed to meet a Nun in the hotel café. She will provide documents that will get him and the children into Canada. In return, Otto will supply intelligence to the *Sinarquistas* contact in Toronto, who will pass it on to the German embassy in Mexico City. The Nun is a member of the *Unión Nacional Sinarquista*, the Nazi-leaning, Catholic extremist political party and an acolyte of Hellmuth Oskar Schleiter, a German agent and member of the Nazi Party.

The Nun appears carrying a brown envelope in one hand and a colourful fabric doll in the other. Otto stands to greet her. He can see she is young with what would be a pretty appearance if it wasn't for the long red scar that runs down the right side of her face. She joins Dace and the children. She hands Dace the envelope. "Everything you need is in the packet: visas, funds, and the name and address of your contact in Toronto."

She holds up the doll. "Your daughter must be frightened. This might help." She hands the doll to Florence.

Otto: "Nothing for the boy?"

The Nun shakes her head. "He's a boy. Why would he want a doll?"

Heinz grabs the doll from his sister. He thrusts it up towards the Nun's face. *"Flittchen!"* He throws it on the ground. Florence runs to retrieve it.

Otto: "The children need sleep. They've had a long and tiresome journey."

The Nun scowls at the little boy. "A beating would be more useful." She gets up and walks away.

That evening Otto sits at his hotel room desk with a small sewing kit and his trench coat in front of him. Florence stands beside him, clutching her new prized possession; she loves her present and her Papa. Otto takes a knife from his pocket. Florence watches while Heinz sulks on the bed. Otto slits the lining of his coat and removes a brown leather pouch. He opens the bag and takes out the pink diamond. He holds it up so Florence can see it.

Florence: "*Wunderschön!*"

Otto smiles. "Yes, my dear, very pretty."

Heinz jumps up and runs to the desk. He grabs the diamond from his father. "*Es ist meins!*"

Otto takes the jewel from his son. "*Nein!*"

The boy shuffles back to the bed to sulk some more. Otto takes the doll from his daughter. He slices open the back to create a gap; he can see the tears well up in his daughter's eyes. Heinz smiles as he watches his sister's distress. Otto kisses Florence on the forehead. He takes the diamond and puts it back in the leather pouch; he stuffs the bag into the hole he made in the back of the toy. Otto sews up the back of the doll, sealing the diamond inside. He hands the repaired toy back to Florence. She throws her arms around her father and kisses him.

Otto: "Be very careful with the doll. Hold on to it tight. Never let it out of your sight." The little girl nods up and down as dramatically as she can.

Heinz snarls, "*Flittchen!*"

Chapter 2
Axel and the Asshole

Present Day

Ivars Dace wipes his brow with a white silk handkerchief for the third time. He stuffs the silk back into the breast pocket of his suit jacket. I doubt it will stay there long.

Axel: "You nervous, Dace?"

Dace: "You unnerve me, Mr. Axel." He pulls out the damn puff again and wipes non-existent sweat from his forehead. I lean back in my chair. Put my feet up on the desk and grin. It's the type of grin that betrays little friendship. "It's either Mr. Webb, Axel, or hey-you, not Mr. Axel. Got it?"

He pays no attention to my smart-ass comment. Instead, he reaches into his jacket pocket. The sudden movement causes me to quickly remove my feet from my desk and stretch for the top drawer, home to my pals, Smith and Wesson. I stop. He drops a white envelope on my desk, causing a fan of hundred-dollar bills to spill out. I caress the cash like it's a lover's inner thigh.

Dace: "Now who's nervous, Mr. Axel?"

I ignore him. Ivars Dace is a seedy little man with a Peter Lorre accent and a nervous, obsequious manner. He is a servile, nasty little prick, but the stack of hundred-dollar bills laid out on my desk demands attention, something I rarely muster without some incentive.

I am an impatient person. Perhaps that's why I have few friends and a phonebook full of enemies. Confronting people about their hidden vices and recently revealed misdeeds does not get you nominated for Mister Likability. I have a tendency to be abrupt, especially with characters I don't like, people like Ivars Dace.

Like most clients that find their way into my inner sanctum, he has secrets. He is not what he pretends to be. The item he wants me to track down is a diamond, a fucking large pink sucker weighing in at one-hundred-and-thirty-three carats.

Dace: "If I may, Mr. Axel, just as a warning." Do you believe this? The little *putz* is threatening me. "Mr. Axel, if you try to keep the prize, sell it, or perhaps hang it around the neck of that pretty creature that decorates your front office, well, then I would have to kill you. Do you understand, Mr. Axel, kill you dead?"

Axel: "Sure, I get it. I keep the gem; you kill me or at least try. It's been tried before. If you want, you can check that out for yourself. All you have to do is visit the Mount Pleasant Cemetery."

Dace: "That isn't very funny, Mr. Axel. I am a serious man with serious associates. They would be quite unhappy to find me dead."

Axel: "Serious associates: interesting." I figured the little creep had backers. He doesn't have the wit, or the balls, to do this on his own. He's merely the frontman. "Well then, I guess we are both on notice."

Dace: "So, we do understand each other."

Axel: "Okay, Dace, I get it. You lost something, and you want it back. Maybe you did lose it, maybe you never had it, or maybe it belongs to someone else. Not my business. You're afraid I'll keep it, but that's not my style. Rocks that size are always more trouble than they're worth. You got some dough, and you're prepared to part with it. And that's just fine with me."

Dace: "Excellent!"

Axel: "So you think this stone is in the city. Why here? Why not Antwerp or Israel?"

Dace: "The Fat Man is here, and the Fat Man wants it. He swears it's the Savola Diamond; he knows where it's hidden. He claims it's a family heirloom. Now he wants to cut it into smaller stones and sell them off. He needs the money."

Axel: "This Fat Man, have a name? And an address would help."

Dace: "The Fat Man has many names. I can't tell you what he calls himself now. When I knew him, he called himself Amadeus Savola. Says he's some kind of Italian Count. I understand he's frequently seen having supper at a steak house downtown called, The Flapper's Club."

Axel: "Well, that's a place to start. I always enjoy a good steak." I pause. "Understand, the envelope is only a downpayment. It doesn't include my expenses."

Dace: "Indeed, Mr. Axel, indeed, plus expenses and a substantial bonus when you find it."

Axel: "You called it the Savola Diamond. What's that all about?"

Dace: "I wouldn't know. It's what the Fat Man calls it. It's just a marketing gimmick to jack up the price. It's not important."

Axel: "I doubt that very much. Now, if you'll excuse me, I have a rock to find."

Chapter 3
Axel and the *Contessa*

The following morning, I show up at the office early. JoJo is already there, and the coffee is brewed. Instead of her usual casual greeting, I get a more formal, "Good morning, Mr. Webb." Her eyes dart to the three ordinarily empty chairs that comprise my front office decor. I turn to see an attractive woman in one of the seats. JoJo rolls her eyes as if to warn me of what's coming. The woman jumps from her seat and charges me like a wounded calf seeking protection, "Thank god you're finally here."

Damn, and here I thought I was early. The woman stands so close I can feel her body under the fabric of her outfit. She lingers, pressed against my chest. If she was any closer, we'd need to get a room. JoJo smirks at the obvious second-rate theatrics. She's seen it all before: a frustrated woman with a philandering husband and a near-empty pocketbook. Canadians call them purses, but a four-year stint in Red Sox country taught me all about pocketbooks. I'm a Blue Jay fan now.

Axel: "Perhaps we should take this into my office." She nods with a rather pathetic lip-biting quiver. JoJo reaches up from her desk with a tissue in a decidedly sarcastic gesture, "Tissue, my dear?" I scowl at JoJo's insolence. I think it's why I love her. I lead the woman into my office and close the door.

Woman: "I don't think your secretary likes me."

Axel: "Don't mind her; she's very protective. And she's not my secretary." I point to the backwards writing on the window behind my desk: *Axel Webb & Associates*. "She is my associates."

Woman: "I see."

Axel: "So, Miss…"

Woman: "It's *Contessa*, *Contessa* Charlotte Savola."

If every woman claiming to be a *Contessa* or deposed Princess were true, they would outnumber us plebs. This woman had the looks and style, albeit just a little frayed at the edges, but I like that in a woman. Most people wouldn't notice these things, but most people aren't me. She has seen better times.

She is attractive and certainly worthy of a closer inspection. She appears to be young or at least youngish. Old enough to have been around but not old enough to be used up. Sure, that's sexist, but it's also accurate. She wears an expensive, black baggy designer pantsuit with a matching vest with nothing underneath. The fabric could not conceal her slim yet ample assets. Her initial greeting introduced them to me firsthand. She is quite the dish; a dish that can cause heartburn if you're not very careful.

Axel: "*Contessa*, is it? I must be moving up in the world. Perhaps I should raise my prices." I pause. "Did you say your name was Savola?"

Contessa: "Why? Has that bastard been here?"

I give her a look. "Language, my dear *Contessa*, language. I'm shocked."

She turns off the broken sparrow act, revealing her true self. "I doubt that men like you are bothered by such language."

Axel: "You peg me as a tough guy, and maybe I am. My clients prize results over sophistication which is why you're here. That said, I know lots of bastards. You'll have to be more specific."

Contessa: "Yes, that's true. I need a hard man. A hard man who's not afraid to get his hands dirty."

Axel: "Just to be clear. I may not be a saint, but if you're implying, I do things that could get me locked up. You'd be very much mistaken."

That's bullshit, as I am sure you already know. I've done a thing or two the authorities wouldn't approve. That's why people come to me and not some uptown firm.

Axel: "You didn't answer my question."

Contessa: "You didn't answer mine. But yes, my name is Savola. Now tell me. Did my fat-ass husband contact you?"

This is getting interesting.

Axel: "You must understand, *Contessa*, my clients rely on my discretion. But if you were a paying client, I might tell you who hasn't contacted me."

She fumbles in her purse, looking for something. She finds it, dropping a wad of hundred-dollar bills on my desk. I don't budge. Who says the cashless economy has arrived. My eyes move from the money to her face. She smirks, "Now I'm a fucking client."

Axel: "No fat-ass husbands."

Contessa: "What about my brother?"

Axel: "And who might that be?"

Contessa: "Ivars Dace. You'd remember him. A little weasel with a nervous manner."

Axel: "I'm afraid not: no one matching that description. Business has been kinda slow lately." So I lied, sue me. "Tell me, *Contessa*, what can I do for you and your stack of Robert Bordens?"

Contessa: "There is a stone, the Savola Diamond. It's been passed down to each succeeding *Contessa* for hundreds of years until the beginning of WWII. In 1940 the stone was turned over for safekeeping to a Swiss lawyer, my Great Grandfather, Otto Dace. During the war, Grandad disappeared along with the diamond. He and the diamond were traced to Argentina, where the trail was lost until last year when rumours of a large pink diamond made the rounds. You can imagine the interest something like that would create. One-hundred-and-thirty-three carat pink diamonds don't grow on trees. The Savola Diamond is my diamond. I am the *Contessa* Savola. And I want you to get it back. I'll pay you one percent of its value if you get it back for me."

Axel: "The fat-ass husband in question is Count Savola?"

Contessa: "Yes, *Conte* Savola."

Axel: "And, precisely, what would one percent of its value be?"

Contessa: "Pink diamonds that size with an interesting history can sell for hundreds of thousand of dollars per carat. The Sakura sold for almost thirty million. And it was slightly less than sixteen carats."

Axel: "So, what if fat-ass divorces you and remarries? Wouldn't she be entitled to the diamond?"

Contessa: "Sure, but he's not getting remarried. I won't give him a divorce, and we're Catholic. Besides, he's fat, ugly, and gay. No woman would have him. I should know. Besides, he loves me."

Axel: "I'm sure there are a few women around that would forgive the *Conte's* peccadilloes in exchange for a multimillion-dollar diamond."

Contessa: "I didn't even know the diamond existed. Becoming a *Contessa* seemed worth the trade-off of marrying such a man. He pursued me. He wasn't so bad back then. Unfortunately, he was always gay. In retrospect I realized he thought I had the diamond because I'm a Dace, but I don't. My brother thinks he's entitled to it. He says it is a family heirloom, but the truth is Great Granddad stole it. But now, I am the *Contessa* Savola. And I am rightfully entitled to it."

She gets up from her seat and comes around the desk to my side. She stands over me as she leans back on the desk. She touches my arm. "You aren't the cynic you pretend to be, Axel Webb. I can see you are conflicted. They've been here, haven't they? They hired you to find the diamond, but it's my diamond."

She moves to the door, puts her hand on the knob, and turns. "I don't see you returning my money. One percent pays a lot of rent, Axel." She smiles, "Plus, you'd have my eternal gratitude. So do what you're good at, and find it."

She leaves.

Chapter 4
The Flapper's Club

I leave JoJo at the office to dig into the backgrounds of Ivars Dace and the mysterious Amadeus Savola. While JoJo does the hard work, I visit The Flapper's Club for a medium-well-done steak with a side of information. The restaurant is located downtown on Elm Street. It's an elegant, stylish Art Deco joint, favouring chocolate brown wallpaper with gold geometric patterns. The chairs are rich medium blue velvet mini tub chairs on casters. If you aren't careful when you sit down, you could end up in the kitchen or on Elm Street.

A large painting of a flapper in a sexy chocolate brown and gold dress with obligatory fringes and matching headband hangs on the far wall. All the waitresses are wrapped in the same signature speakeasy outfits, hence the name, The Flapper's Club.

The maitre d' is a woman in her middle-to-late thirties. She wears a white satin tuxedo and open-neck black silk blouse. Her hair is bobbed, blonde and animated. She's a knockout.

She smiles with a broad but professional greeting, "Mr. Axel Webb, I presume, table for one?"

Axel: "Yes, thank you."

As she leads me to my table for one, she asks, "First time at The Flapper's?"

She already knows the answer, but I respond just to be polite. "Why yes. Nice of you to notice."

Maitre D': "Well, I do hope you become a regular like many of our other guests."

Axel: "If the food lives up to the quality of the staff and the environment, I might just move in."

She smiles a generous smile. She's used to men flirting and knows how to deal with them. "You are a cad, Mr. Webb. I best be careful of you." She winks, taking the sting out of the crack. She places the menu in front of me, a brown leather folio with a gold embossed flapper on the cover. "Someone will be with you in a moment. In the meantime, I'll get you our signature cocktail, compliments of the owner."

Axel: "And exactly who would that be?"

Maitre D': "Why I am, Mr. Webb." She turns and leaves. A few minutes later, she reappears with my drink. She places it in front of me. I notice she delivered the cocktail personally and not by one of her minions. "For your approval, Mr. Webb."

I take a sip. "Not bad. Normally I prefer vodka over gin, but this isn't bad. What is it?"

Maitre D': "We usually serve guests our complimentary, *Mary Pickford*, but I felt that just wasn't your style. So, it was a tossup, either *The Southside* or the *French 75*. That..." She points to the drink on the table. "... is a French 75."

Axel: "Why those two, and why the *French 75*?"

Maitre D': "Well, Mr. Webb, they say, The Southside was Al Capone's favourite drink. But, you don't strike me as a gangster. The French 75, on the other hand, is named after a dangerous quick-firing gun. Both are dangerous; both are lethal, and; both are things to be careful around." The woman *ain't* so bad at flirting herself. "Tell me, Mr. Webb, why are you really here? And I have a very well-developed bullshit detector."

I hand her my card, "Please, sit, and I will reveal all." She hesitates but only for a second. She sits, looks at the card, and then at me.

Maitre D': "Axel Webb & Associates, 11 Tank House Lane, Toronto, Ontario. Usually, gentlemen's cards say what they do, lawyer, accountant, undertaker."

Axel: "Well, I'm no gentleman and not every job is so easily defined. But if you need a definition, let's say I find things for people."

Her face goes hard. "You're a private investigator... a Dick!"

Axel: "Shamus, flatfoot, gumshoe, there are lots of names you can call me, and I've been called them all."

She sits back in the chair and sighs. I watch her blouse move up and down, betraying her outer calm. "What do you want, Axel? I'm a busy woman."

Axel: "We're making progress. I've progressed from Mr. Webb to Axel. So my beautiful new friend, what's your name?"

Maitre D': "My name is Katrina Klein. Now, if you don't mind, I can use the table for a real customer."

Axel: "I am a real customer. I want a centre cut top sirloin, medium well done, and baked potato with everything but sour cream."

Katrina: "You say you find things. Like what?"

Axel: "Now that's a complicated question. There seems to be a what and a who. Tonight, I'm looking for the who, a Fat Man, that goes by Amadeus Savola."

She leans forward over the table. I can't help but notice she isn't wearing anything under the black silk; it's a trend I could get used to. She watches my eyes but doesn't object. "The *Conte*, he comes in three, maybe four times a week. He wants something, like you." She sits back in her chair. One of her staff approaches, but she waves her away. "What do you want with him?"

Axel: "I don't really know. Information, I guess. He's looking for the same thing my clients are. And everybody says it belongs to them. But nobody seems to have it. As far as I know, it may not even exist."

Katrina: "This thing everyone is looking for, it's worth a lot of money?"

I nod. "A very lot of money, if what they say is true, but I don't believe a word anybody says. I'll bet it's like the Guan Yu rubies, a legend, a story people tell of a lost treasure. They almost always turn out to be fairytales for people that don't want a real job." She smiles; it's like winning a stuffed animal at the CNE.

Katrina: "Sounds like you have more than one client."

Axel: "I do."

Katrina: "Isn't that unethical or something?"

Axel: "Or something." She smiles again.

Katrina: "Since you have rather flexible ethics, how about adding one more client to your list?"

Axel: "You?" She nods. "How can I resist a woman who buys me a fancy drink named after a lethal weapon?"

She stands. "Find out what the Fat Man wants."

Axel: "And when I do?"

Katrina: "Stop him. I'll get you that steak and a retainer for your services."

Chapter 5
The Hunt Begins

Cascais, Portugal, 1947

The abdication of the King turned Italy into a Republic with a new constitution that forced descendants of the House of Savola to leave the country. Since the Republic of Italy turned its back on the aristocratic family, *Conte* Luca Umberto Savola had no choice but to flee to Portugal.

Conte Luca, his wife, *Contessa* Gianna, and their newborn son, *Contini* Amadeus, find themselves guests at the *Palacio Seixas* with dwindling bank accounts and an urgent need to locate Otto Dace and their one-hundred-and-thirty-three carat legacy.

Conte Luca makes inquiries at the Our Lady of Assumption, where he writes a cheque for a substantial donation he can't afford, only to be told to go to a nearby café and wait. The *Conte* finds a table on the café patio and sits. Forty-five minutes pass without anyone showing up. It's bad enough to be strong-armed by the Church for a donation he can't afford, but now it feels like he's been stiffed. An elderly widow dressed in black makes her way to his table. Luca is about to stand, but she motions for him to sit. She stops at the table, looking down at *Conte* Luca.

Widow: "*Conte* Luca?"

Luca: "*Sì.*"

Widow: "A Nun will meet you on the *Palacio* patio overlooking the water in one hour. They say the view is beautiful." She moves away, not waiting for an answer.

The *Conte* gets up and leaves. One hour later, Luca finds himself perched on the parapet of the patio *Palacio Seixas* overlooking the rocks and water below. A Nun approaches. She walks with purpose, directly to where Luca is sitting. Luca stands. He can see she is young and not unattractive, except for the nasty scar that runs down the right side of her face.

Nun: "You are Luca Savola?" The *Conte* is peeved she doesn't use his title, but he can't afford to act superior. He needs to find Dace and his goddam pink diamond.

Luca: "*Sì.*"

Nun: "You need to get to South America? It will cost. And I understand you're short of funds."

Luca: "I just gave the Priest a big cheque."

Nun: "That was for the Church. This is for the cause." Luca knows about the cause, but politics and religion no longer hold any interest for the *Conte.* The only thing Luca is interested in is finding the pink treasure.

Luca: "I have no interest in going to South America unless that's where I can find Otto Dace."

Nun: "You're looking for Dace? Why?"

Luca: "I gave him something valuable to hold on to during the war. He never returned it, and now he's missing."

Nun: "This something valuable; what is it?"

Luca: "That's my business." The Nun smirks and turns to leave, but Luca grabs her shoulder. She stops. "It's a diamond, a very large diamond." He doesn't realize his hand is still on the Nun's shoulder. The Nun looks at his hand on her shoulder, then into his eyes.

Luca: "*Scuse!*"

The Nun peers down at the rocks below; she watches the Atlantic as it slaps the jagged shore. Luca has remained standing at the edge of the parapet the whole time.

The Nun turns away, gathering her momentum, while she scans the patio for guests. There are none. She wheels back towards *Conte* Luca Umberto Savola, pushing him over the wall. The force of her sudden action is so strong Luca doesn't have time to scream. The sound of his body splattering across the rocks below is masked by the Atlantic engulfing the former Italian aristocrat's remains.

Chapter 6
Searching For Clues

After dinner with the lovely Katrina Klein, I head back to the office. It's late, but JoJo is still hard at work with a stack of orange grade school exercise books at the ready. She prefers to use the schoolgirl aid over scraps of paper. The books help JoJo keep track of all her random notes, thoughts and avenues of inquiry. She'll eventually organize the information into an official report on the computer, pretty enough to present to a client. There is something about the visceral act of putting pen to paper that helps arrange the puzzle into a meaningful picture. It may not be particularly efficient, but it works.

I grab a coffee and make myself comfortable behind my desk. JoJo takes her usual position in the chair across from me. We have our way of working, and we stick to it. JoJo says I'm anal about things like that, and to be honest, I can't argue the point. She begins her report without a preamble. "The *Conte* Amadeus Savola, otherwise known by some as the Fat Man, is the only son of *Conte* Luca Umberto Savola and *Contessa* Gianna. According to what I could gather from English newspaper records, *Conte* Luca committed suicide by throwing himself off the patio of the

Palacio Seixas. If you can believe the reports, he was distraught over the loss of his official aristocratic status, not to mention being asked to leave Italy and not come back, an order that stayed in place until the early 2000s. Other more colourful journals blamed money for his depression, specifically the lack of it, and one even suggested foul play, although no suspect was mentioned."

Axel: "Anything about this Savola Diamond everyone seems to be after?"

JoJo: "Aah, yes, the pink diamond. Some reports conclude the loss of the Savola Diamond pushed old Luca to take the dive, but others say the whole giant rock thing is bullshit, a legend. But, *Contessa* Gianna swore it was real and that it was stolen by a Swiss lawyer who was supposed to keep it safe during the war. The *Conte* feared the Fascists or Nazis would grab it, but he got screwed anyway."

Axel: "Did the *Contessa* ever mention who this Swiss lawyer happened to be?"

JoJo: "I guess you won't be surprised to learn that the *Conte's* Swiss lawyer was Otto Dace."

Axel: "Well, of course, it was. And he must be our client's Grandfather or something."

JoJo: "Otto is Ivar's Great-grandfather."

Axel: "So Ivars figures, Great-granddad squirrelled away the gem someplace and like the squirrelly bastard he was, he forgot where he put it. Kind of unlikely if you ask me. People just don't misplace one-hundred-and-thirty-three carat gemstones. So, were you able to trace what happened to Ivar's *mishpachah?*"

JoJo: "Partly. It seems Otto and his two kids made their way to Buenos Aires and then Mexico City, then he disappears, later, to reappear in our fair city where he is killed in a traffic accident. The reports are conflicting. Some witnesses swear he was pushed in front of a streetcar, while others say he tried to make it across King Street without looking. In any case, he got hit and died, and the whereabouts of the pink prize died with him."

Axel: "So Ivars and the current *Conte* think Otto hid the diamond somewhere in the city, and they are here to track it down."

JoJo: "So it seems."

Axel: "So what happened to Otto's kids?"

JoJo: "They went to an orphanage. The little girl was adopted within the year, but the boy remained in the home until he was fifteen, when he ran away. That is where the trail stops."

Axel: "Keep digging. Ivars must be the Grandson of the boy. Obviously, he doesn't have it. Maybe Otto stashed the diamond with his little girl. See what you can find out."

JoJo: "I'll get into it tomorrow. Anything else?"

Axel takes Katrina Klein's cheque out of his pocket and puts it on the desk. JoJo picks it up.

JoJo: "Another new client?"

Axel nods. "Katrina Klein, she owns The Flapper's Club."

JoJo: "And what does she want you to do for her?"

Axel: "Stop the Fat Man."

JoJo: "Stop the Fat Man doing what?

Axel: "Your guess is as good as mine."

Chapter 7
Don't Forget The Doll

The Lobby of the Royal Alex Theatre, 1947

O n his arrival from Mexico City, Otto got a job as a paralegal for the Royal Alex arranging contracts with the acting companies that come to the historic playhouse to perform. He ignored the Nun's instructions to contact the local German agent. Otto had no interest in the Nazi cause and wanted nothing to do with the *Sinarquistas*. He assumed the local agent got caught or escaped. In any case, the war was over, and the danger had passed. Or so he thought.

He was safe in Canada, with a decent job and a bright future for his family. The diamond would provide the financial means he needed to take advantage of the inevitable post-war boom. Soldiers returning to civilian life created an enormous demand for all goods and services. Staying in Buenos Aires made no sense. Coming to Canada was the right move. He is determined to take advantage of the opportunities the diamond could provide.

In the meantime, the pretty flapper doll sits perched on Florence's nightstand in her bedroom in his rented house. It's five o'clock, and the afternoon matinee is about to conclude. He wants to leave before the rush-hour chaos begins, but the telephone rings. He instinctively answers it. He should have ignored it. Now he'll be caught in the dash for the exits.

Standing in the lobby pretending to study the seating chart for a coming attraction is a Nun: a very pretty young Nun except for the nasty scar that runs down the right side of her face. If the *Conte* was correct and Otto Dace had the precious stone, she would get it.

The *Sinarquistas* need to be financed, and the diamond would fund their cause for years to come. She'd be a hero, more than a hero, a miracle worker, a *Sinarquista* leader.

Dace leaves his office and heads for the street. The Nun pushes her way through the Royal Alex patrons, all racing to catch the next King streetcar. She catches up to Dace and takes his arm; her grip is firm. They walk west along King Street towards Simcoe. "You never made contact."

Otto: "I have no intention of getting involved in your religious and political scheming. I have a new life, and I'm not going to risk it on a lost cause perpetrated by fanatics."

The Nun is livid, but she holds her temper. "The deal was we get you out of Mexico to Canada, and in return, you supply information to the cause."

Otto: "I'm a paralegal; I deal with contracts for acting companies. I had nothing to do with the war effort. I couldn't, and I won't, help you."

Nun: "Well, what about the diamond."

Otto's blood runs cold. "What diamond?"

Nun: "The Savola Diamond, the pink beauty you stole from the *Conte* and smuggled out of Switzerland, that diamond. The diamond you will deliver to me as compensation for your broken promise."

Otto: "What kind of Nun are you? You're an evil Nazi bitch, and I'll never give you a thing. Never!"

He pulls his arm away from the Nun. The Nun's temper erupts. She pushes Dace hard towards the street. He stumbles, not able to keep his balance. He falls in front of the on-coming eastbound King streetcar.

Passing pedestrians scream in horror seeing the Swiss lawyer's body hurtling through the air into the westbound rush hour traffic. The Nun disappears in the ensuing chaos.

Cumberland House, Toronto, 1948

Mr. and Mrs. Sharpe arrive at Cumberland House to pick up their new twelve-year-old daughter. The Sharpes are Jewish immigrants from Germany who were wise enough to get the hell out of the Fatherland before Hitler came to power. Florence and the Sharpes are a perfect match. The little girl's new family owns a thriving Elm Street restaurant, and they speak German. Where they live is filled with young children Florence's age, including thirteen-year-old George Klein, who would eventually become Florence Katrina's husband and the grandfather of the owner of The Flapper's Club.

Mrs. Henderson, the Director of Cumberland House, enters the girls' dormitory to fetch Florence. Mr. and Mrs. Sharpe wait in Mrs. Henderson's office. Florence sits on her bed beside her packed suitcase clutching her prized doll close to her chest. She loves her cloth flapper doll, and despite her young years, she knows the value it hides inside its cotton-batten innards.

Mrs. Henderson looks at Florence and smiles. "I see you haven't forgotten your stuffed friend. I've never seen a girl your age so attached to a doll. God forbid you left it behind, but I'm sure your new parents will buy you lots of new toys. And you'll have plenty of friends to play with. Pretty soon, you'll forget all about that silly doll. Now come along; your new parents are waiting."

As they enter Mrs. Henderson's office, Heinz Victor barges in. He grabs the doll from Florence, shouting, "Mine! The *Flittchen* is mine. Papa wanted me to have it." He tries to make his escape, but Mr. Sharpe, Florence's new Dad, grabs him by the shoulder. He takes the doll from the boy and hands it back to the little girl. Florence hides behind Mr. Sharpe's leg, protecting herself from her violent and volatile brother.

Mr. Sharpe: "Young man, I doubt your father gave you a doll to play with. I understand you are disappointed to see your sister leave, but if you behave, I am sure Mrs. Henderson will find you a nice new home."

Heinz Victor: "I hate her! I hate this place. The *Flittchen* is mine, and one day I'll get it back." He stomps off down the hall.

Chapter 8
Nun of Your Business

Present Day

This is the third night in a row I will have the pleasure of consuming a French 75 while watching Katrina Klein preside over her epicurean domain. Tonight, she wears one of her sumptuous signature satin tuxedos. In truth, it's Katrina that's sumptuous; the wardrobe is merely her prop. Ms. Klein and I have developed a relationship beyond client and gumshoe. This evening I am greeted with a kiss; and a black number set off by an open-neck white silk blouse featuring K-shaped diamond-onyx cufflinks, accenting the sartorial flourish of her jacket's surgeon's cuffs. They say dining is about pleasuring the senses, and Katrina Klein delivers as much sensual pleasure as any man can handle.

Katrina: "You're in luck; he's here. I've seated him in the back where it's quiet. There are only three tables in that section. A Nun has the one behind him." She puts her hand on my back and steers me towards the Fat Man. Now that I see him for the first time, I can confirm the man is a whale.

When we arrive at the *Conte's* table, Katrina stops. "My dear, *Conte*, may I present Mr. Axel Webb. I believe he is interested in Italian history and would love to buy you dinner." The introduction is perfect, except for the *buy you dinner* part, but I'll just put the expense on Katrina's bill.

I admit this wasn't exactly my plan, but Katrina is as clever and cunning as she is attractive. She wants to know what he wants from her, and my job is to stop him from getting it. For all I know, he just likes the food.

Conte: "You'll excuse me for not getting up, Mr. Webb, but as you can see, the effort might prove overwhelming. Please sit."

Katrina: "The usual Mr. Webb?"

Axel: "Yes, thank you, My Dear." She smiles a genuine smile. The My Dear is not just a familiarity aimed at Katrina, but notice to the Fat Man, she is under my protection. He smiles graciously, understanding my intent.

Conte: "It is a pleasure to finally meet you, Mr. Webb." He beams a fleshy elephantine smile. "Oh, don't look so surprised, Mr. Webb. I know my wife has paid you a visit."

Axel: "She isn't the only one interested in your misplaced diamond."

Conte: "I'm not surprised. My wife's brother is also on the hunt." He stops to think, considering his next move. "Interesting..."

Axel: "That her brother is after the diamond?"

Conte: "No, Mr. Webb; that you come right out with it, a boldface acknowledgement. It's a style I can admire... as long as it doesn't get in my way."

Axel: "First things first, what do you want from Katrina?" I hoped my blunt demand sounded personal rather than official. Whether it was for Katrina or myself remains to be seen.

The *Conte* tries to sit back in his chair, but his bulk forces him forward. "Aah... so you don't know as much about our hostess as you think you do, how very interesting. Perhaps you've been played, my friend. The Savola Diamond belongs to the House of Savola, and as head of the family, the diamond belongs to me. It was stolen by my wife's Great Grandfather. And I want it back."

Axel: "My understanding is the diamond belongs to the *Contessa* Savola, so, in actuality, it belongs to your wife, not you."

Conte: "A minor technicality, I assure you. It belongs to the Savola family. She is merely the temporary caretaker. Besides, my wife has come back to me. She occasionally likes to feign independence, but she enjoys being a *Contessa,* almost as much as the riches the diamond will provide."

Axel: "What do you know about Katrina that you think I don't?"

Conte: "A lot, I am sure, but why be coy. Katrina is the key to finding the diamond, which I will explain in good time. For now, let us understand one another. My wife hired you to find the diamond, which means I hired you to find the diamond. You see, we've come to an agreement of sorts. As I am sure she's told you, my preference in the area of romance leans in a different direction, which I understand can be quite frustrating for someone like my wife. But as a concession, I've agreed to provide an heir, ensuring continued ownership of the jewel if my Charlotte remains my wife, at least in name. As I said before, she likes being a *Contessa,* and she likes money. She can have both if she stays married to me. Of course, we have to find the diamond."

Axel: "You're aware her brother is also a client?"

Conte: "Oh yes, I am aware. A bit of an ethical co-
nundrum, but I am sure you will manage to
straighten that out, unless..." His voice trails off
while his eyes move over my right shoulder to
watch Katrina seat a well-dressed man at the
Nun's table. I don't turn to look.

Axel: "Something wrong?"

The *Conte* tries to refocus on me, but he is still
obviously distracted. He regains his composure.
"Ivars Dace is an insignificant little man with big
ambitions, but a man who lacks the wherewithal
to achieve them."

Axel: "That is something we can agree on. I believe he's just the frontman for someone more
powerful and perhaps more dangerous."

Conte: "Yes, you are correct. And the instrument
of that danger is sitting at the table behind you."

Axel: "The Nun?"

Conte: "The Nun, indeed. And her associates. Be
careful, my friend. She is not what she appears to
be. She wants the diamond, and like all religious
and political fanatics, she'll do anything to get it."

Axel: "So she's been following you for a while?"

Conte: "Not just me, Mr. Webb. She's following you as well. I suggest you dispose of her quickly. Perhaps with the help of your associates, Smith and Wesson."

The comment is disturbing; it could be a mere coincidence; then again, perhaps not. "A Nun? You want me to whack a Nun? That's a bit harsh, don't you think?"

Conte: "I suggest you study some Mexican history, with special attention given to the UNS."

Axel: "The UNS?"

Conte: "The *Union National Sinarquista* or just the *Sinarquista* for short. But for now, tell me why Katrina hired you?"

Axel: "That's my business, *Conte*, but I can tell you this. She isn't interested in me helping her find the diamond."

The *Conte* laughs so hard he almost knocks over the table with his large belly. "My dear Axel, she doesn't need you to find the diamond: she's the one who has it."

Chapter 9
Triangulation

The *Conte* finishes his thousand-calorie dessert. But before saying goodnight, he reminds me that he and the *Contessa* are now an entry. As such, he expects to be kept abreast of developments. I adjourn to the bar to watch the Nun and her dapper dinner partner. He is a handsome forty-something character with a swarthy complexion and black slick-backed hair; he brings to mind the *Conte's* comments on Mexican history and the *Sinarquista*.

I call JoJo to check in and have her follow up with the *Contessa* to confirm the *Conte's* claim of unity. It would not surprise me the Fat Man is looking to freeload on his wife's investment. JoJo tells me the *Contessa* already called to inform us she has reconciled with the *Conte*. Talk about your marriage of convenience. I asked JoJo to do some research on the *Sinarquistas*.

JoJo asked if I thought it was a good idea to have her boyfriend, Marco, a former Argonaut linebacker from UCLA, tail Dace. I agreed we have a lot of balls in the air and too many clients to keep track of all by myself. She said she'd look after it, but I knew she already had Marco on the case.

Marco Octavio Menendez is a menacing fellow you wouldn't want to meet in a back alley. The former CFL football player was too small for the NFL but more than big enough for the Canadian game. After a decent career, he decided to stick around, mainly because of JoJo, poutine, and Timmy's double-doubles. Despite looking like a villain that just stepped out of a Marvel comic, the man is a pussycat.

I down the last of my second French 75 and order another from the friendly bartender. "Barkeep, can you bring me another?" He nods.

I notice a small black and white photograph on the wall behind the bar. It's an elderly couple standing in front of the newly renovated Flapper's Club. Both are stylishly dressed despite their advanced years. The man wears a nicely tailored dark custom suit, Borsalino hat, and a pleasant smile. The woman wears a long black silk dress and gold necklace; she leans on a black ebony cane with an oversized baseball-styled knob as a handle. She must have been a knockout in her younger days. She has a striking resemblance to Katrina.

The bartender places a clean coaster on the bar along with my cocktail. "Just curious, have you worked here a long time?"

Bartender: "Doesn't seem like it, but yes, a very long time. I used to work for the Kleins before Katrina renovated the place and turned it into The Flapper's Club."

Axel: "That photo of the older couple behind the bar, are they Katrina's parents?"

Bartender: "Sure, that's Mr. and Mrs. Klein, lovely people. You couldn't ask for better bosses. And Katrina is just like them."

Axel: "So that's Katrina's mother?"

Bartender: "Yes, that's Florence. She was a wonderful lady."

Axel: "She had a bad leg?"

Bartender: "I guess." The bartender sees my reaction to his odd response. He leans over the bar and almost whispers. "That's kind of a funny thing. When she came out of her office to greet customers, she used the cane and had a noticeable limp, but when I went into her office to give her the weekly liquor order, the cane was always on the stand beside her desk, the limp was gone, and she moved like a track star. I always found that curious. I figured the cane was an affectation. No one ever got angry with Florence. They'd see the cane and cool off immediately, no matter how mad they were. Nobody wants to yell at a limping old lady." The bartender winks and goes back to work.

I nursed my third French 75 while keeping an eye on the Nun and her dinner partner. Katrina comes over to see how my encounter with the *Conte* went. "Did you find out what he wants?"

Axel: "Yes, in fact, I did."

Katrina: "Are you going to tell me?"

Axel: "He thinks you have the Savola Diamond."

Katrina: "That's the treasure you mentioned when we met?" I nod. "Why would he think I have it?"

Axel: "Well, do you have it?"

Katrina looks me in the eye. "I like you, Axel. I like you a lot. I want to be honest and tell you yes or no, but the answer is not that simple. Why don't we put that question on hold for now."

Axel: "That's okay by me, but if Dace or the *Conte* think you have it, you could be in danger. And there's something fishy with that Nun you sat behind the *Conte*."

Katrina's face goes white. "Did you say someone named Dace is after this stone?"

Axel: "Ivars Dace, a little weasel, who's fronting for someone who is after the diamond."

Katrina: "Meet me at your office tomorrow around ten o'clock. We have to talk." She kisses me on the cheek and goes back to work.

I finish my drink just as the Nun and her friend finish their supper. I try to pay my bill, but Katrina won't take my money. I leave the restaurant and settle in my car to wait. A taxi pulls up just as the Nun and her friend exit the restaurant. They get into the cab and drive off with me following close behind.

I follow through heavy downtown traffic. I'm told 416 traffic can compete with any major metropolis and not in a good way. The cab pulls up in front of a New York-style brownstone in the Church and Wellesley area. The reddish brick three-story with decorative brick portico complements the black stone steps that lead to a charcoal wood and glass door with *El Club Latinoamericano* neatly painted in gold on the glass. I park several townhouses down the street and watch as the Nun and her friend enter. I hear a tap on my passenger side window. I look; it's Marco. I unlock the door, and Marco gets in.

Marco: "If I'm going to stake this place out, I should have brought snacks. I'm still learning the finer points of being a Private Dick." He chuckles and taps me gently in the arm. "That's PI humour." And he laughs again. "Why are you here? I told JoJo I'd follow the little prick."

Axel: "You followed Dace here?"

Marco: "Yeah, he went in about fifteen minutes ago. Did JoJo call you?"

Axel: "No, I followed the Nun and her boyfriend that just went into the club."

Marco: "Wow, Nun's have boyfriends. She must be a member of a very progressive order." I look at Marco. He chuckles, "I crack myself up."

Axel: "Yeah, something like that. Listen, Marco, can you wait them out and let JoJo know when they leave and where they go."

Marco: "Sure, no problem, but it will cost you."

Axel: "Okay, what do you want?"

Marco: "A double-double and two apple fritters from Timmy's."

Axel: "Your fee has gone up, but I think I can manage it."

I head to Timmy's for Marco's coffee-and-fritter run. I deliver the snack to Marco and phone JoJo to get her opinion on putting Marco on the payroll full-time. I also ask her to do some research on the *El Club Latinoamericano*.

Things are starting to take shape, and that shape is a triangle. The *Conte* and *Contessa* occupy one point of my three-sided dilemma, Dace, the Nun, and her Mexican pal crowd the second, and Katrina occupies the third. I am having trouble reconciling on whose behalf I am working. I took money from Dace, the Contessa, and Katrina, but not all sides of this triangle are equal. If I'm honest, Katrina is the one I'm rooting for.

Chapter 10
The Mexican Connection

The Nun and the Mexican enter *El Club Latinoamericano* and go directly to the lounge. The club bar is all dark wood panelling and brown oiled leather. The carpets are reddish-brown without a noticeable pattern laid over dark stained wood flooring that matches the wall panelling. A formidable four-by-eight painting of the *Unión Nacional Sinarquista* founder, Salvador Abascal, hangs on the far wall with a photo of Nazi intelligence agent Hellmuth Oskar Schleiter displayed on one side; and an image of an elderly Nun with a nasty scar on the other. An oversized red, white, and green UNS flag hangs on the opposite wall.

Ivars Dace sits in the corner in a dark brown leather Georgian-style Wingback chair. Dace fiddles nervously with his drink. He pulls the white silk puff from his suit jacket pocket and wipes his brow. The Nun and the Mexican take the two matching Wingbacks opposite.

Mexican: "When did you get here?"

Dace: "About fifteen minutes ago. So, did you find out anything?"

Mexican: "Nothing we didn't already know."

Dace: "So, it was a waste of time."

The Nun cuts him off. "You really are a fool, you little man."

Dace tries to defend himself. "Now, just one minute. You can't talk to me like that. You wouldn't even be in the game if it wasn't for me."

The Nun reacts angrily. "Listen, little man, you're nothing, your Great Grandfather was a thief and a liar, and if you're not careful, you will suffer the same fate."

The Mexican reaches out and touches the arm of the Nun. "We are all allies here. Our cause is just, and our path is clear. We must take possession of the stone. It is God's plan and the means for us to implement the Lord's revolution. *Viva Cristo Rey.*" The Mexican and the Nun raise their glasses and drink. Dace reluctantly follows their lead.

Nun: "The *Conte* was there with that private investigator. And the woman seemed very cozy with him, too cozy."

Dace: "My cousin has the *Flittchen*. It must be in the restaurant somewhere. It's obvious."

Nun: "We don't know that for sure. The Nun glances toward to photograph of the scar-faced Nun. "Sister Cristero had a temper. She had your Grandfather killed without first finding the diamond. It was a mistake."

Dace: "Exactly. Without me, you'd be lost. I know the diamond is hidden in the *Flittchen*."

Mexican: "Good to know. So, what's a *Flittchen*."

Dace: "It's German for hussy... you know, a floozy, a slut. My Grandfather had dementia; he was obsessed with the damn *Flittchen.* He never shut up about the thing; it was always Florence and her *Flittchen*; it made me sick. What do you expect; the man was crazy?"

Nun: "Yeah, big help."

Mexican: "Well, at least it's a direction. We find the *Flittchen*; we find the diamond."

Chapter 11
The Girls' Club

I arrive at the office to find JoJo and the *Contessa* discussing something serious over freshly brewed coffee. I pour myself a cup, and we adjourn to my office. JoJo knows better than to confide in the *Contessa.* I assume she is pumping her for information. Or perhaps, it is the *Contessa* that is operating the pump. "You girls mind telling me what is so interesting?"

The *Contessa* sits back in her chair, letting JoJo do the talking.

JoJo: "Charlotte was telling me..."

I interrupt. "It's Charlotte, is it? I better keep a close eye on you two. Before I know it, you ladies will be hitting the Magic Mike shows together."

Contessa: "Don't be jealous, Axel. You can strip for us anytime." JoJo laughs.

Katrina: "Oh really? I've arrived just in time for the show." We turn to look. Katrina stands in my office doorway with one hand on her perfectly formed hip. She wears a black linen pantsuit and open-neck black silk blouse. I am stunned at how attractive she is and how closely she mirrors the *Contessa*, who is almost as beautiful. The three women eye one another like vultures, circling a carcass, looking for the best parts.

I grab an extra chair from the outer office for Katrina. In the time I'm gone, the three women have become pals. They are laughing and smiling, mostly, I suspect, at my expense. How much is real and how much is an act remains to be seen. Whatever comes next is bound to be interesting.

I take the seat behind my desk, partly because it's the only other chair in the room and partly for protection from the newly minted scallywag sisters sitting in front of me. "Well, ladies, I am not sure where we should go from here."

Katrina: "I have a suggestion."

Contessa: "Go ahead, *Cuz.* I'm all ears."

Katrina: "I don't understand."

Contessa: "You don't know, do you?" Katrina shakes her head. "My maiden name is Charlotte Dace. I'm the Great Granddaughter of Otto Dace, the man who stole the Savola Diamond."

Katrina's eyes go wide, but she remains other-wise calm. "So we are cousins."

Contessa: "That's right, my dear, and that little prick, Ivars, is my religious nut brother. And the Nun and her Mexican friend who were at your restaurant last night are his associates. They want to get their hands on my diamond, and they'll do anything they have to do to get it, in-cluding murder."

Katrina: "Murder?"

Contessa: "The Nun, and her friend, are members of some crazy fanatical right-wing religious or-ganization. I believe that group is responsible for the murder of Amadeus' father and our common patriarch, Otto Dace."

JoJo: "I can confirm some of that. I've been look-ing into the UNS and *Sinarquista* movements. Without getting too deep into the weeds, the *Sinarquistas* were, or are, a political-religious movement that calls for the return of Catholic influence and Catholic values in Mexico, along with some right-wing fascist ideals. It grew out of the Cristero Rebellion, whose advocates objected to the secular and anticlerical elements in the Constitution of 1917. The conflict ended in 1929, but fascist groups, Nazi sympathizers, and

Catholic radicals joined forces in 1937 to form
the *Unión Nacional Sinarquista*."

Katrina: "What does that have to do with Otto
Dace and Charlotte's father-in-law?"

JoJo: "It seems one of the leaders of the most rad-
ical faction of the movement was a scar-faced
Nun who was rumoured to be involved in the
murders of *Conte* Umberto and Otto Dace. The
woman was a Nun, so no one in Portugal or
Canada believed she would commit one, let alone
two, murders."

Katrina: "So why was she involved with Otto
Dace in the first place. He was Swiss, wasn't he?"

Contessa: "Yes, he was. Evidently, Umberto gave
Otto the diamond to hold for safe-keeping during
the War, but Otto took the diamond and his two
kids, my Grandfather and your Grandmother, to
Argentina. In Argentina, Otto hooked up with a
Nazi agent who got him to Mexico City and later
Toronto. In return, Otto was supposed to supply
intelligence to the Nun. In turn, she was supposed to pass it on to the Germans. Otto refused,
so they demanded the diamond instead. He had
no intention of giving up the diamond, so they
killed him. Of course, all of this is conjecture, but

at least it provides some context for what is happening now."

Katrina: "All that is very interesting, but what has it got to do with me? If I had this Savola Diamond, I would know. And I don't."

Axel: "I might have a solution if the diamond still exists, and we can find it."

We hear muffled arguing from the front office. The door flies open, and Ivar Dace is catapulted through the office door onto my oriental rug.

We look up from the startled Dace to see the substantial figure of Marco Menendez filling the door frame. "Sorry for the interruption, but I believe this little prick wanted to see you." He closes the door, but before anyone can react, he re-opens it. "Let me know if he gives you any trouble. I'll watch the front office." He closes the door.

I get up from behind my desk and drag Dace to his feet. I brush off some imaginary fluff from his shoulders and pull his ever-present white silk puff from his jacket pocket. I dab his brow gently. He ungraciously grabs the handkerchief from my hand and stuffs it back in his breast pocket. He pushes me backwards. He turns to see who else is in the room. He notices the three women.

Dace: "What's going on here?" He takes a step back. He points to the women, "Why are they here?" He practically screams the words, but they sound more like a whine. He looks at me. "You! You bastard! You're in cahoots with these sluts."

Axel: "Cahoots, aah, I haven't heard that one in a while, but now that I think about it, it's not a bad idea. You have to understand, the ladies are far prettier than you. And, they offered me more money. So why don't you just run along? Maybe you can find a Nazi Mexican Nun's shoulder to cry on."

Dace is near apoplectic. He reaches into his jacket and pulls out a SIG Sauer P365. He waves the micro semi-automatic around like a deranged Cab Calloway on Speed. "I'll kill you, Webb! I'll kill you dead, understand, dead!"

Axel: "Yeah, I get it. You'll kill me dead; usually that's how it works out. You said your piece, so why don't you put that peashooter away and go home?"

Dace steps towards me and raises the gun to shoot, but I hit him with a hard right. He starts to fall backwards from the blow, but I grab him by the collar with my left hand and slap him back and forth with my right. I don't know how many times I hit him, but it was enough to make his eyes roll back into his skull. I release his limp body and let it fall. When his gun hand hits the floor, he instinctively pulls the trigger. The women dive for cover. The office door flies open, and Marco rushes in. He sees Dace's body lying in a heap in the middle of the room. JoJo, the *Contessa*, and Katrina are piled one on top of another, with Katrina on the bottom.

Axel: "Was anybody hit?"

The girls untangle themselves and scramble to their feet. I don't see any blood, but my desk sustained a leg wound. Katrina tries to take a step forward but crumbles. I catch her before she falls. She looks up at me: dishevelled but still beautiful. "My knee, I must have banged it on the floor." I help her to her seat.

JoJo retrieves the gun. "The fool didn't have the safety on. I think we better hold on to it."

Axel: "Marco, it's time to take out the trash? Dump this clown in the elevator and press sub-basement."

Marco: "There is a dumpster in the alley. I could drop him there. We can still make today's garbage pickup."

Marco picks Dace up by the scruff of his neck one-handed and drags his semi-conscious body out of my office. I retake my seat and look at the three women. "Okay, then, where were we?"

After a brief inspection to see if everyone is still in working order, we discuss how to proceed. We decide to reconvene at The Flapper's for dinner.

Chapter 12
The Flapper's Rapprochement

I pace Katrina's office like an expectant father waiting for his wife to deliver a decade-and-a-half of trouble. Her office is all mahogany and ebony with an inlaid hardwood floor that looks like it was lifted straight out of some nineteen-twenty movie mogul's office. The entire Flapper operation reeks of money, and Katrina's office is no exception. Either the restaurant is doing exceedingly well, or the missing Savola Diamond somehow found its way into the extraordinary Art Deco decor of The Flapper's Club.

While we wait for Katrina, I enjoy the view of Charlotte Dace Savola, the *Contessa*, making herself comfortable in one of the two tub chairs opposite an extraordinary Ruhlmann desk.

Conte Amadeus occupies most of the Hansens three-seater on the opposite wall. Behind the desk is a mahogany and ebony wall unit that looks like it was designed by Mondrian. The shelves are filled with leather-bound volumes except for one odd ancient memento: a vintage flapper doll that today would be considered unsuitable for children.

Marco waits in his car across the road from the restaurant in the event the Mexican connection makes an appearance.

At precisely eight o'clock, Katrina enters the office wearing her signature black satin tuxedo, but with the addition of her Grandmother's black ebony cane. She is obviously feeling the effects of this morning's misadventure. She haltingly makes her way to the desk and takes her seat.

Katrina: "I apologize for keeping you waiting: restaurants don't run themselves." She motions towards Axel. "You called the meeting. Why don't you begin?"

The *Contessa* visibly straightens in her chair while the *Conte* remains splayed on the couch as if waiting for some peasant boy to peel him a grape. His breathing is laboured. He gives the impression that repositioning his substantial self-animating flesh might cause a stroke.

Contessa: "Take your pills, Darling. We wouldn't want you to drop dead in Katrina's office before she has a chance to give us back our diamond."

The *Conte* tries to answer but instead retches and coughs till his face turns blue. Charlotte jumps up and goes to her husband. Katrina and Axel look on, unclear if Charlotte's concern is genuine or strategic. Katrina buzzes the bar for someone to bring a pitcher of water. Charlotte reaches into Amadeus' jacket pocket and pulls out a yellow pill bottle. "Amadeus, take the goddamn pills." He opens his mouth and sticks out his tongue. Charlotte puts a pill on it. The bartender arrives with the water. He hands a glass to Charlotte, who gives it to the *Conte*. He drinks. The colour starts to return to his face.

Charlotte hovers over the *Conte*, concerned. Obviously, there is more affection between them than they admit.

Conte: "I'm fine. It's nothing. Just a little heart condition." Charlotte touches her husband's cheek. He kisses her hand. "I'm all right, my Dear. Perfectly fine. Please, let's move on." Charlotte hesitates, but Amadeus waves her off. She returns to her seat. "Axel, please continue."

Axel: "I believe we may be able to find common ground despite the apparent obvious mistrust."

The *Conte* tries to lean forward, but the attempt isn't worth the effort. "The Savola Diamond is mine. That is not in dispute."

Contessa: "Actually, the Savola Diamond belongs to the *Contessa* Savola, and I happen to be the *Contessa* Savola."

Katrina: "I don't have your diamond. And if I did, I'd give it back. I don't need it. And I don't want it. I'm successful, doing what I do. I don't need some museum piece that makes me a target for every conman and thief in the city."

Contessa: "So, you have no idea where it is or who has it?"

Katrina: "None." The room goes silent.

Conte: "But you don't refute the fact that Otto Dace stole it?"

Katrina: "If you say he stole it. I believe you, but I only heard about it when Axel told me you believed I had it."

Conte: "We know Ivar doesn't have it, so Otto must have given it to your Grandmother. She must have told you something."

Axel: "Otto could have stashed it somewhere for safekeeping. He was hiding it from the Nun and her Nazi friends. It could still be sitting under a floorboard in someone's apartment. Or, it could have ended up in a garbage dump when the hiding place was demolished. After all, it was a long time ago."

The *Contessa* looks at Katrina: "Your mother never mentioned a pink diamond or some family treasure?"

Katrina tries to stand; Axel goes to help. He hands her the cane. Katrina hobbles to the bookshelf and takes down the flapper doll. She walks over to the *Contessa* and gives it to her. "This was my Grandmother's great treasure."

Katrina takes the doll from Charlotte and moves to the *Conte*. "You want it; it's yours." The *Conte* shakes his head. Axel helps Katrina back to her chair; he is obviously concerned about her leg. "The doctor said my knee will be fine in a few days. Please put this back on the shelf?"

Axel looks at the doll carefully. "What's the story with this doll?"

Katrina: "My Grandmother would never let the doll out of her sight. She said she got it in Mexico before she came to Canada. She told me it would make me a fortune. Look around; the doll is the inspiration for The Flapper's Club. The restaurant is my fortune, not some pink rock. I think

Axel is right. The stone is probably buried under eighty years of garbage in a dump somewhere."

Axel looks at the *Conte*. His breathing hasn't improved. "Charlotte has offered me one percent of the stone's value if I find it. I suggest you make the same deal with Katrina."

Katrina: "I like money as much as the next person, but I'd be happy if you can just get the religious fanatics and political crazies out of my restaurant and my life."

Axel: "Understood, but if we are going to trust one another, we all have to have something at stake. It's human nature. What do you say, *Conte*, one percent for me and one percent for Katrina?"

Amadeus hesitates.

Axel: "Ninety-eight percent of something is better than one hundred percent of nothing. And if the rock is worth anywhere close to what you estimate, the two percent is mere pocket change."

Conte: "I'd hardly call two percent of millions of US dollars pocket change."

Axel: "Maybe not, but a million bucks *ain't* what it used to be, but the choice is yours. There is no guarantee I can find it. But, if any of us do find it, the deal stands. If we can't agree on that, I walk. I'm good with finding my new favourite restaurant." Katrina smiles.

Conte: "What do you think, Charlotte?"

Contessa: "Axel's right. Best we all work together instead of at odds with one another."

Conte: "Fine. We have a deal."

The phone on Katrina's desk rings. She picks it up. "Yes… a break-in… when… I see… I'll be right there." She hangs up the phone. "That was the police. Someone broke into my apartment and ransacked the place."

Axel: "It had to be Ivars or the Mexican."

Katrina: "Axel, do you mind taking me home; it's hard for me to drive."

Axel: "No problem. I'll want to talk to the cops anyway. Perhaps it's time to let them know about these people." He turns to Charlotte, "My associate has been waiting outside watching for the Nun and her friends. I'll have him take you and the *Conte* back to your hotel."

Chapter 13
The Flapper Must Die

The Nun and Ivars sit in a car watching Marco. They wait for the Mexican to call. The Nun's mobile rings. She answers. "Is it done... Good... Are the cops there? Excellent." Ivars touches the Nun's shoulder. She looks towards where Ivars is pointing. She sees Marco rush into the restaurant. "Wait a minute, something is happening. The cops must have called."

The front door of the restaurant opens a couple of minutes later. Axel and Katrina appear. Katrina holds Axel's arm while balancing herself on a cane in her other hand. Axel helps her into his car. Marco exits the Club steadying the *Conte* with the *Contessa* on his other side. He squeezes the *Conte* into the backseat of his car and helps the *Contessa* into the front. Both vehicles drive off in different directions.

Nun: "Okay, they've left the restaurant. We're going in now. The bitch must have hidden the stone in her office. We'll meet you back at the hotel."

She hangs up and drops the phone into the cupholder. "You distract the staff while I pretend to go to the restroom. Wait for me at the bar. If anyone heads for her office, call me."

Ivars: "Then you better take your phone." She picks up the phone and slips it into a pocket in her habit." They get out of her car and head for the front door of The Flapper's Club.

The Nun casually makes her way to the Ladies' Room while Ivars annoys the assistant manager. Halfway to the restroom, the Nun changes direction and heads for Katrina's office. She's lucky the door is unlocked. Either Katrina always leaves her office unlocked, or she forgot. In either case, the Nun was able to just walk in. She uses the fabric of her habit to turn the doorknob; she doesn't want to leave any fingerprints. Once in the office, she slips on a pair of latex gloves: making sure no DNA is left behind.

She surveys the office. Her face contorts into a sarcastic smirk. She mentally estimates the cost of the furnishings; *'This stuff must have cost a fortune. I might be too late. Maybe the diamond has already been sold or recut into smaller stones, each worth a tidy sum. The smaller diamonds would be easier to sell without drawing too much attention. Smart... very smart.'*

The Nun pulls open the drawers of the Ruhlmann desk, scattering the contents on the floor. She finds nothing. She takes a painting from the wall, checking for anything hidden in the back. Nothing. She throws the canvas on the carpet. She stops and looks around the room, scanning for possible hiding places.

She rips all the cushions from the tubs chairs and sticks her hand into the crevices to see if anything is hidden. She is getting more frustrated and angry by the minute. She takes a knife out of her habit pocket and violently slits open the cushions. Nothing. She proceeds to the Hansens three-seater and does the same thing to it, nothing again. She stops to scrutinize every possible hiding place. The weirdly configured bookshelf is all that's left to search. Maybe the prize is hidden in one of the leather volumes neatly displayed on the shelves.

She goes to the fancy wall unit and starts grabbing books, throwing each one on the floor after searching for false pages. She rips open the last book but finds nothing. She angrily tosses it across the room. It ricochets off the wall and knocks over an elegant Tiffany-style glass Art Deco lamp; it shatters as it hits the floor. She smirks in defiance.

The flapper doll sits lonely on the shelf. She stares at it, tilting her head like a hound trying to interpret her owner's command. "The doll! The sexy flapper doll!" She says it out loud. "Ivars' fucking *Flittchen*!" The bitch has hidden the diamond in the doll. She grabs the flapper from the bookcase; she takes the knife she used to rip open the chair cushions and uses it to cut a hole in the back of the doll. She splays open the back and rips out the cotton batten guts. Nothing.

Nun: 'FUCK!" Then almost under her breath: "Fuck! Fuck! Fuck!"

She looks at the knife in her hand. No, she can't use that. She spots a bronze letter opener shaped like a flapper on Katrina's desk. She picks it up with one hand while squeezing what's left of the flapper doll in the other. She pauses. She positions the childhood keepsake in front of the bookcase and drives the letter opener through the heart of the flapper, crucifying it on the Mondrian-styled wall unit. The Nun smirks one more time. She admires her handiwork. "Next time, bitch. Next time, it will be you!"

Chapter 14
One Dead Doll

atrina and I arrive at her suite at the Botsford Hotel to find the place busier than Union Station at rush hour. The Botsford is one of those New York-style luxury boutique hotels with several permanent guests; one of them is Katrina Klein. Uniform patrolmen, detectives, and CSI-types do their best to make an even bigger mess than whoever broke in. Not that it is a state secret; it had to be one, or all three, of the *Mafiosos Mexicanos Nazis*. Katrina couldn't figure out how they managed to get past security, but a Leafs' game on television is all that is needed to distract minimum wage rent-a-cops. The ranks of hotel security guards aren't filled with former CSIS professionals. Around three AM, the yellow tape went up, along with instructions to find Katrina a different hotel. We end up at the Four Seasons in Yorkville.

We talk, drink, and stare at each other while our blood pressures find normal levels. Katrina pushes hard to discover the inner Axel Webb while I do my best to fake it: there are things about me that I prefer she doesn't know.

Katrina: "You know I'm pretty smart for a broad."

I smile at the self-deprecating, anti-feminist self-characterization. "Yeah, you're pretty smart, period, but I can't tell you what I don't know."

Katrina: "Or maybe, you're just too comfortable being a loner."

Axel: "I don't pay too much attention to the guy that stares back at me in the mirror; I think it best to eliminate the navel-gazing and move on."

Katrina: "While I like what I see. And you can put money on me finding out who you are, whether you tell me or not."

Axel: "I wouldn't bet against it, Sweetheart. In fact, only a fool would bet against you." She smiles, gets up from the bed and kisses me.

We talk a little longer and agree to meet in her office after lunch. That gives us both a few hours' sleep. I insist Marco picks her up and hangs around until this deal is done. She needs a chauffeur anyway, and nobody with half a brain will mess with her as long as Marco is nearby.

Later that morning, Marco calls from the restaurant. There was another break-in. This time it's Katrina's office at The Flapper's Club.

When I get to the club, it's a rerun of the Botsford fiasco. I see Marco standing off to the side while Katrina speaks to one of the detectives. Marco motions me over.

Marco: "It's a mess, boss. They really did a job on the place."

Axel: "I can see."

Marco: "I'll be in the dining room, keeping an eye on the front. Holler if you need me." I nod.

I look at Katrina. I can see the salty puddles pooling in the corners of her eyes. I take her hand and squeeze; she leans against me. It feels good, very good.

Katrina: "They destroyed the place." I don't respond. What can you say? I squeeze her hand tighter, trying my best to be reassuring. "They even mutilated my Grandmother's doll. What kind of freaks do a thing like that?"

Axel: "It's psychological warfare; either that or whoever did it is crazy."

Katrina: "I vote for crazy."

Axel: "Obviously, they were looking for the diamond. They must have thought your Grandmother hid it in the doll."

Katrina: "That makes sense. Maybe it was Ivars? Gran told me her brother, Heinz, hated that doll. He called it a *Flittchen*. Even as a child, Heinz was a prude. He must have passed on his crazy to Ivars. And that whole side of the family is obsessed with the damn diamond. Even Charlotte is plagued by the thing. Why else would someone so beautiful marry a man like the *Conte*?"

Axel: "*Flittchen*, it sounds German."

Katrina: "It is. It means hussy or floozy, you know, a slut. The guy was nuts."

The damage to the restaurant is isolated to Katrina's office. The rest of the restaurant is fine. The staff didn't notice anyone entering the office, but the Assistant Manager said he was distracted by some irritating little man that sounded a lot like Ivars. He must have kept the staff busy while one of his associates trashed Katrina's office.

The whole operation is starting to sound like it was orchestrated. The Mexican breaks into Katrina's apartment to search for the diamond. He doesn't find it, so he calls the cops, telling them he hears noises in his neighbour's suite. The Mexican hightails it before the cops arrive, but before he leaves, he calls the Nun and Ivars, who are watching the restaurant waiting for us to rush out. That gives them time to search Katrina's office. They may be nuttier than a drunken band of *Lucha Libres*, but they're not stupid.

When the cops finish questioning the restaurant staff, Katrina starts preparing for the dinner rush. I send Marco home to get some rest with instructions to pick Katrina up in the morning. I hang around the bar to keep an eye on things.

Chapter 15
"Bei Mir Bist Du Shein"

"I've tried to explain, bei mir bist du schein,
So kiss me and say you'll understand."
Songwriters: Jacob Jacobs / Sammy Cahn /
Saul Chaplin / Shalom Secunda

The following morning I go to the office to check in with JoJo. Everything is copacetic, so I head on over to the restaurant. When I arrive, I see Katrina stuff a wad of cash into a manila envelope before handing it to a fellow with a tape measure attached to his belt and a flat carpenter's pencil jammed up over his ear.

Katrina sees me enter; instead of her usual warm reception, I receive an ever-so-slight narrowing of her penetrating brown eyes. She recovers quickly and smiles. She turns back to the contractor. "And make sure everything is perfect: exactly how it was."

Contractor: "Everything will be perfect, Miss Klein. Don't worry."

Katrina: "One more thing." She turns and pulls the still impaled *Flittchen* off the bookcase. She hands it to the contractor. He looks at her as if to say, '*what do you want me to do with this?*'

Katrina: "I want it repaired and framed... with the letter opener through the doll's chest."

The contractor looks at the doll and then at Katrina. "But..."

Katrina doesn't let him finish. "Just do it! Or I'll find someone else who will. Understood?" I haven't seen this side of Katrina before; I shouldn't be surprised. A businesswoman who survives in the restaurant racket must be hard, or she'll get swallowed whole. The contractor leaves, and Katrina visibly relaxes. She looks at me and smiles. "Good morning, handsome." She tosses me her Granny's cane from across the room. "Eureka! I'm cured. The leg feels fine. No more cane. Nice catch, by the way."

Axel: "Well, I did use to be a ballplayer."

Katrina: "Really? I told you I'd eventually get to know the real Axel Webb. A ballplayer, my goodness, were you any good?"

Axel: "All glove, no bat."

Katrina: "You are a man of many talents."

Axel: "So what's with '*Bob the Builder*?' Aren't you going to wait for the insurance adjuster?"

Katrina: "I refuse to look at this mess any longer than I have to. If the insurance company gives me a hard time: I'll switch companies. I didn't get to where I am by letting myself get pushed around by pencil pushers."

Axel: "I can see that. And that doll business with the contractor, what's that all about?"

Katrina: "A little reminder to myself, so I remember what can happen if I'm not ahead of the game." She can see my reaction is more than a bit surprised. Have I been overly mesmerized by her beauty? I've let my professional guard down? Is Katrina Klein a lot more, and a lot less, than I thought? Women like Katrina have always been my kryptonite. I twist the cane in my hand, realizing she's upset me.

Katrina: "Come, I'll have the kitchen make you something to eat." She starts to move to the door; her limp is barely noticeable. She sees me analyzing her movement. "I told you, I'm fine. The leg will be back to normal in a few days. I don't like the customers seeing me with a cane." She looks at me, strangling the ebony walking stick."

Katrina: "What? It's just a cane."

Axel: "Tell me, did your mother drink?"

She turns to look at me. I can see she is bewildered by my question. "Why yes, she did like her Schnapps, especially Berentzen Apfel. We always had some in the restaurant. Why do you ask?"

Axel: "This cane... I've run across walking sticks like this before. It's a flask cane."

Katrina: "You must be wrong. Why would she need a flask cane? The bar was always fully stocked. That's how we make money."

I walk over to Katrina's desk. "Maybe, it was used to hide something: like a large pink stone that certain people were willing to kill to get their hands on."

Katrina: "That's crazy, Axel. I'll bet this whole diamond nonsense is a scam. I'll bet there is no Savola Diamond and that there hasn't been one since the beginning of WWII. *Conte* Umberto probably sold it; then claimed Otto Dace stole it so he could get the insurance money. A nice double payoff scam."

I unscrew the ball-shaped handle on the walking stick while Katrina theorizes about the diamond's existence. Before she finishes, I dump five unused vials on her desk; vials meant to carry prohibition booze. She looks at the vials and picks one up. "These vials are far too narrow to hold a diamond the size of the Savola, and besides, they're empty."

Axel: "Have you ever seen a cane with a handle that looks like a baseball?"

Katrina: "I don't know. I'm not a cane expert." She is close to anger. "What are you suggesting?"

Axel: "I'm not suggesting anything. I'm telling you, nobody makes a cane like this. It's difficult to hold, especially for older folk with arthritis."

Katrina: "My Grandmother never had arthritis."

Axel: "Exactly. She purchased this cane because of its odd design. She bought it to hold this." I pull a brown leather pouch from the hollow baseball-sized handle.

Katrina's eyes go wide. I empty the contents of the pouch onto her desk. It's a large pink diamond worth a shitload of dough.

Axel "You knew, didn't you?" She tries to talk, but I don't let her. "You had the fucking diamond all the time. That bullshit about I don't want it, I don't need it, it's more trouble than it's worth, are all lies. Your Grandmother gave that stone to you, and you used it for collateral. Everyone wondered how you turned your grandparents' little restaurant into this place." I point to the stone. "That's how."

Katrina: "Axel, please, let me explain. Please, you don't understand."

Chapter 16
The Handoff

I got played by a pretty face, again. It's not the first time and probably not the last. I walked out of The Flapper's Club determined to write the whole sordid mess off. Halfway back to the office, I cooled off enough to call Marco and tell him to keep doing what he was doing, which he found odd because I hadn't told him to stop. Katrina still needed protection from Ivars and his band of miscreants; besides, she did pay me. To be honest, I still have a thing for the woman despite realizing she isn't the innocent I imagined her to be.

Back in my sanctuary, I fill JoJo in on my new theory of the case. She makes me realize that I might have jumped to a conclusion and that maybe, just maybe, Katrina is telling the truth about not knowing the diamond was hidden in the cane. I'm not sure I believe it, but JoJo does make me feel better.

Once the emotional cobwebs cleared, I had a better picture of my obligations. I got in trouble by taking money from three people with opposing agendas. I've already eliminated Ivars and his Mexican Nazi bandits; that leaves Katrina and the *Contessa*. Katrina hired me to discover why the *Conte* was hanging around and stop whatever scheme he had up his pudgy sleeve. Meanwhile, the *Contessa* hired me to find the diamond and secure it. It appears I've accomplished all my obligations, except for the final handover of the rock. JoJo reminded me we still had a one percent finder's fee on the line, but will Katrina give up the diamond?

I had no intention of strong-arming Katrina. But if she refuses to turn the rock over to the *Contessa,* we'll have a problem. On paper, the diamond rightfully belongs to the *Contessa.* Whether that would stand up in court is always a gamble.

I had JoJo arrange a meeting with Katrina and the Savolas at our offices, neutral ground. JoJo tells Katrina to bring the diamond. It's time to put a pin in this assignment and move on to something with uglier women and less emotional complications.

I sit in my office studying the backwards lettering on the window overlooking The Distillery District. It reminds me of Sam Spade's office, but I'm no Bogart, and I have better furnishings. I hear JoJo arguing with someone in the front office. I get up to find out what the trouble is, but before I can reach the door, it opens, and JoJo comes flying into my arms. I catch her before she hits the carpet.

Axel: "You okay, kid?"

JoJo: "I'm fine. The little creep gets pushy when he doesn't get his way." JoJo rearranges herself, deftly straightening her skirt and tossing her shoulder-length jet black hair. My eyes move to the doorway. The little creep in question is Ivars Dace.

Ivars: "You took my money on false pretences. You had no intention of finding my diamond."

Axel: "Your diamond? I believe the *Contessa* Savola is the rightful owner."

His mouth opens to speak as he takes an aggressive step in my direction. "That stone is…" I hit him with a hard right. He goes down like Angel Di Maria of Real Madrid, but there's no one to give me a red card.

JoJo looks down at the inanimate slab that is Ivars Dace. "I think you killed him." She gives him a swift kick in the ribs with her pointy-toe heels. He groans.

JoJo: "Guess not. Too bad, I wouldn't mind being a witness for the defence. I'd look pretty good on the stand, don't you think?"

Axel: "JoJo, my dear, you always look good. Just don't tell Marco I said it." She smiles and heads back to the front office.

Ivars starts to come to life. He manages to roll over onto his knees. He gets to his feet with some difficulty. He sways back and forth like a drunken sailor on a bender. "I think you chipped a tooth."

Axel: "Too bad, I was trying to knock it out."

Ivars: "You hit me in the face." He says it like he's surprised.

Axel: "That's what I was aiming for."

Ivars: "Why does my side hurt?"

Axel: "JoJo kicked you with her pointy shoes. You really shouldn't mess with the lady."

Ivars gradually puts his brain cells back in order, "I'll get you for this, Webb. You took my money and knocked me around twice. You won't get away with this."

Axel: "What are you going to do; get your Nazi Nun girlfriend and her Mexican pimp to come after me? It's a done deal, daddy-o. The Fat Man and his *Contessa* have left the building and taken the rock with them." This wasn't remotely true, but I was working on it. "Now, get the hell out of my office before I call my pals at 51 Division." That is also a load of twaddle since the local constabulary doesn't know me from a used crash test dummy.

Ivars has gone down for the count twice. The look in his eyes demand vengeance, but the pain in his face and gut urge caution. He waves a haphazard fist in my direction and stomps out.

Based on JoJo's conversation with Katrina, it appears she is willing to turn over the diamond to the *Contessa*, who is historically the rightful owner. Her one percent finder's fee would be some consolation for the loss of the rock, especially if she didn't know it existed.

JoJo already had my lawyer draw up contracts stating that Katrina Klein and Axel Webb and Associates would receive one percent of the proceeds each from any sale or distribution of the Savola Diamond or any smaller gemstones created from said diamond.

All concerned, arrive at the appointed time. The meeting runs smoothly and quietly without much banter or small talk. Everyone is polite, but a pall of tension hangs in the air like a precursor to disaster. Katrina keeps looking in my direction. It is her way of making a peace offering. I tried a smile which she responded to, but that was the extent of our communication. The deal was done. The Savolas got their diamond, Ivars got a black eye, chipped tooth, and sore ribs, while Katrina and I might eventually get a big payday, not that I would put money on it.

Something just didn't feel right. Why would Katrina give up a multimillion-dollar diamond for one percent? She's too savvy to settle for such a small return. I'm missing something, something big; I need insurance. I call JoJo into my office. "JoJo, get me Raffy Reinhardt on the phone."

JoJo: "Raffy? What's up? Why bring him into this? The deal is done, isn't it?"

Axel: "Something is off. We need insurance: out-of-town insurance."

A few minutes later, JoJo pokes her head into my office. "Raffy is on line two."

Axel: "Hey, pal, how are you… Ya, me too… How's Charlie, still as pretty as ever… Listen, do you still have contact with those con artists you used to use… Great, wasn't one of them a paperhanger, had a British accent and looked Middle Eastern… Ya, that's the guy. Think he could come up with the documents for a real estate deal? It's insurance, in case I'm being played. You and your friends get ten percent of my end… Set up a meeting and let me know the time and place."

Chapter 17
Easy Come, Easy Go

It's Saturday, and The Distillery District is busy. Ivars stands by the clock tower, drinking a cup of coffee from one of the trendy restaurants in the area. The Nun lingers across the lane, browsing in a shop window; the reflection provides a perfect mirror image of what is happening behind her. She has a clear view of Ivars. Several boutiques further down the street, the Mexican sits on a bicycle watching the tourists window-shop. They wait. They saw Katrina, the *Conte* and *Contessa* enter Axel's building. When they come out, one of them will have the diamond.

It's a simple case of grab, snatch, and disappear. The Mexican will take down the *Conte*, the Nun will grab the *Contessa*, and Ivars will confront Katrina. All three targets exit Axel's building onto Gristmill Lane, heading toward the Clock Tower on Trinity. They make their way to Mill Street, where they can catch cabs. Katrina walks briskly, wanting to get to the restaurant as soon as possible. Like most restaurants, Saturday is the busiest day. She is not happy about how the whole affair ended; she is distracted, thinking of how she can regain Axel's trust. There is definitely a spark between them.

The restaurant is part of her, but Axel's appearance has made her realize there is more to life than work. Her mind wanders as she walks. She pays no attention to her surroundings. She likes Axel; she likes Axel a lot. She wants him in her life, but can she afford to tell him the truth.

Distracted, she walks right into a man. "Sorry! I wasn't watching where I was going." It's Ivars. "You!" Ivars jabs a pistol into Katrina's ribs. He grabs her purse and starts running, but he's clumsy and trips on the uneven cobblestones. Katrina's handbag goes flying. It hits the ground, spilling the contents onto the path.

People start to come to Katrina's rescue. Ivars grabs for the purse, but he runs into a tourist collecting Katrina's things. The crowd increases. Ivars glances at the assorted lipstick, combs, and pens lying on the ground. No diamond. Someone grabs Ivars by the shoulder, but Ivars wheels around, hitting the good samaritan in the jaw with his elbow. Ivars takes off towards Trinity Street to make his escape.

The *Contessa* and the *Conte* are several yards behind Katrina. Amadeus can't move his bulk too fast. He's been having trouble breathing for several days. The excitement of recovering his family treasure has been almost too much for him.

Charlotte sees her brother, Ivars, confronting Katrina. Amadeus is gasping for air. "Amadeus, hurry, there's trouble." Charlotte grabs her husband's hand, trying desperately to drag him into a nearby brewpub, but Amadeus is wheezing and needs to stop.

The Nun hip-checks Charlotte, knocking her to the ground. She grabs Charlotte's purse and starts running. Charlotte scrambles to her feet, ready to go after her, but she sees her husband is in distress. Amadeus grabs his chest and collapses. Charlotte runs to his side and kneels over him. Their relationship may be odd, even unnatural, but he is her husband, and she cares.

The Mexican races up on his bike. He jumps off and goes to the *Conte* as if to help. Charlotte's eyes meet the Mexicans'. He gives her a right cross knocking her backwards. The crowd doesn't help; they are content to video the scene instead of coming to Charlotte's rescue.

The Mexican: "Stand back! This man has had a heart attack. Call an ambulance." The spectators who aren't videoing the incident start to dial 911. The Mexican searches Amadeus' inside jacket pocket. He finds his heart medication. He throws it on the ground. The pills spill out onto the cobblestone path. The crowd tries to pick up the tablets. A few people demand he stop and wait for help. The Mexican ignores them; he reaches into Amadeus' cigarette pocket and extracts a brown leather pouch. He's found it, the diamond, the Savola Diamond. More people are gathering. Shopkeepers come out to see what's going on.

The Mexican jumps up; he grabs his bike and charges into the crowd, scattering onlookers as he runs. He keeps running with the bicycle in one hand; and the leather pouch in the other. Once clear of the crowd, he stuffs the leather pouch into his pocket while simultaneously hopping onto the bicycle.

Axel and JoJo hear the commotion from their office and run to help. An ambulance arrives to take the *Conte* and *Contessa* to Mount Sinai Hospital. Katrina finds Axel. She is shaken but mostly uninjured.

Katrina: "Axel, please get me out of here before the cops arrive." Axel grabs her hand and rushes her back to his office. The diamond is gone, along with the Mexican, the Nun, and Ivars Dace.

Chapter 18
Hold The Pepperoni

There are many ways to kill someone. The gun, favoured by Americans, is efficient and deadly but lacks sophistication. The lack of elegance is characteristic of those that use the weapon. The knife is less efficient and requires more skill and guts as you need to get up close and personal to do the job right. Punching, kicking, and general brawling are inefficient, ineffective, and likely to cause at least as much damage to the doer as the *do-ee*. Strangulation can work, but it requires too much effort. Poison, favoured by women, has a certain charm but is decidedly unsporting.

The Bulgarians prefer umbrellas dipped in something lethal, especially when on vacation in Britain. The Russians don't mind exposing an entire town to radio-active material as long as it does the job. Defenestration has a certain kinetic elegance, but it requires too much planning and can savage your *Feng Shui* if your victim objects. No matter the method, the results are not guaranteed other than to cause a mess and require substantial cleanup. As a result, it is best to do the job out of town at a hotel with a proper cleaning and maintenance staff.

You may find this somewhat bizarre and rather macabre aside irrelevant to our tale, but this is the substance of the conversation that is taking place between the Nazi Nun and her Mexican pal. Ivars Dace, the proverbial third-wheel, lays unconscious in the bedroom, a condition brought on by a double dose of Clonazepam mixed into his rye & ginger by the Mexican.

The *tres chicos malos* are staying in a suite at the YAYS Antwerp Opera Hotel, an establishment that fits the bill as it has an excellent cleaning staff and is out-of-town. The YAYS Antwerp is conveniently located in the bustling Flemish Diamond District. The area is where the Nun and the Mexican hope to turn the pink rock into a substantial pile of greenbacks.

The intended victim of the termination under discussion is Ivars Dace, the odd man out on the *Sinarquista* financial crusade. The two religious and political fanatics see no point in splitting the pink Savola pie three ways when two is preferable. All three partners may have crazy in common, but Ivars lacks the commitment of the other two extremists. Ivars may be a right-wing prude, but he is far more financially driven than politically motivated.

Mexican: "We have to make it look like an accident. We don't want anything coming back to us."

Nun: "Ivars booked the room. As far as anyone can tell, we are just visiting a friend. Did you book the other hotel?"

Mexican: "Yes, I got us rooms at the De Keyser."

Nun: "Well? What do you think? Now is as good a time as any. He's out cold."

Mexican: "We should have dropped a few more Clonazepam in his drink to make sure he never wakes up."

Nun: "I was afraid that would look too suspicious, but you're right; they probably would figure it was a suicide."

Mexican: "It's too late now."

Nun: "We could force a few more pills down his throat. What do you think?"

Mexican: "Risky. We might even wake him up. If he struggles, we're screwed."

Ivars staggers into the room. He grabs his head. "I have a terrible headache."

The Nun gives the Mexican a look. "It's probably jet lag. You should go back to sleep."

Ivars: "What are you guys talking about? Is there a problem?"

Mexican: "Nah, we were discussing which *diamantaire* we should use. The Hasids are the best if you don't mind using a Jew."

Ivars: "Go where we get the best price."

Nun: "Ivars is right. Let's get the best price."

Ivars: "I'm starving. You guys want to share a pizza?"

Nun: "Definitely not. I want real food. There's a nice café around the corner. I think we'll try it."

Ivars: "Fine. I'm not up for a restaurant. I'm just going to order a pizza from room service."

The Nun and the Mexican need privacy to discuss their plan to eliminate Ivars. Dinner may be the only time they have to figure it out. Once the diamond is sold, Ivars will want his cut. He must be dealt with before the sale. The Nun and the Mexican leave Ivars alone to order his pizza. While enjoying a proper meal at the café, they discuss how to remove their problem.

Two hours later, they return to chaos.

The Nun and the Mexican exit the hotel elevator to find the fifth floor filled with cops, paramedics, and guests crowding the hallway near Ivars' room. The Nun turns to one of the hotel guests to find out what happened.

Nun: "What's going on?"

Older Female Guest: "Somebody died."

Mexican: "Who?"

Older Female Guest: "The man in 513."

The Mexican turns to the Nun. "It's Ivars."

The Nun smiles: "It's divine providence; God is on our side. It's an omen."

Older Female Guest: "Excuse me?"

Nun: "God bless the poor soul. Do you know how it happened?"

Older Female Guest: "I heard one of the paramedics say he choked on some pepperoni. Evidently, he vomited all over the place. They'll never get that smell out of the room."

The Mexican nudges the Nun, signalling her it is time to disappear.

Nun: "It's God's will. He's done the work for us. Now, we have to sell the stone, so we can do his work for him."

Chapter 19
The *Diamantkwartier* Disappointment

That evening the Nun and the Mexican search the Internet for an appropriate *Diamantkwartier diamantaire*. They decide it's too risky to go to one of the four top exchanges in the Antwerp World Diamond Centre. They all have impeccable reputations and might ask too many questions, like how a couple of oddball grifters got a hold of the pink beauty. The infamous history of the Savola Diamond is well known in Antwerp's insulated and highly secretive *diamantaire* circle.

The Nun and the Mexican were strange birds at the best of times. But amongst the Hasidic Jews, Jain Indians, and Maronite Christian Lebanese that dominate the Antwerp diamond trade, they were a very odd couple indeed. The decision is made. A smaller, less suspicious firm is needed. One that doesn't ask too many questions; a company that has more interest in profit than provenance.

They found what they were looking for in the *Bourse Aux Diamants De Couleur Fantaisie*, a shop in a nondescript grey building. The building bore none of the upscale embellishments that would

signal a firm dealing in multimillion-dollar trans-
actions. It looked more like a mechanic's workshop than a gem dealer. The entrance is covered
by an unappealing metal garage door. And the
sidewalk out front features a row of motorcycles
and bicycles. Not the kind of transportation you'd
expect of diamond merchants.

The glass door beside the garage entry led to offices above the shop. The owners of the nondescript *Bourse* were a family of Jain Indians. Their
website claims they specialize in dealing with
fancy coloured diamonds, a term used to de-
scribe rare coloured gems that are neither yellow
nor champagne.

The *Bourse* is owned and run by the Dasaani family, headed by the father, Samkit, and expertly as-
sisted by his eldest son, Tuli. When the Nun and
the Mexican arrive, the garage door is up, revealing a more elegant establishment than expected.
They are buzzed into the shop. When the young
woman who greets them finds out the nature of
their business, she directs them to the glass door
beside the shop.

The woman uses a keypad on the glass door to
enter a code; the door opens so the Nun, and the
Mexican, can access the office area. They climb a
narrow staircase to the second floor. They are

blocked by a heavy wooden door with bars and a camera. The Nun is about to knock, but before she can react, there is a buzz, and the door automatically opens. They enter.

The door slams shut behind them. The Mexican turns, startled by the sound of the door closing. They stand in a small alcove that is uncomfortably claustrophobic. In front of them is another door that looks more like a vault. It opens with an eery metallic creak. Standing in front of them is a young man in his middle thirties. He has a medium-dark complexion, jet black slick-back hair, and stylish black titanium glasses. He wears an expensive, custom English-made suit and soft as butter Italian loafers.

Tuli: "Welcome to the *Bourse*. I am Tuli Dasaani. I will be looking after you today. Please, follow me." Tuli ushers them through a busy functional office with four accounting and clerical staff busy working. There is another barred door with a camera that is probably the workshop. They are led into a far more luxurious boardroom with wood-panelled walls, a large solid walnut boardroom table and a set of matching black leather chairs. Tuli casually waves to the chairs. They sit. Tuli takes the seat at the head of the table. He presses a button under the table, and the red recording lights of the four cameras, one in each corner of the ceiling, flash on.

Tuli: "Welcome again, my friends. I understand from my sister downstairs that you have something special to sell."

Nun: "Yes, very special."

Tuli: "Excellent. We are always in the market for a rare gem of exquisite quality."

Mexican: "Pardon me for asking, Mr. Dasaani, but your establishment doesn't look like the kind of place that could afford the stone we want to sell."

Tuli: "Aah, yes, appearances. Well, Sir, appearances can be very deceiving. One assumes a woman wearing a Nun's habit is a Nun, and a man in a nice suit is a man of substance. But are they, my friend? Appearances can be deceptive. Flashy presentation makes a firm a target. We leave that kind of thing to the retailers in the tourist trade. Our business is more..." He searches for the word. "Exclusive. We are more highly specialized than the traditional houses."

Mexican: "I see."

Tuli smiles, doubting the Mexican actually sees at all. "So tell me, my friend, what have you brought me today?"

The Nun reaches into her habit pocket and pulls out the leather pouch. She places it in front of Tuli, spreading her hands apart, palms up, as if in a benediction to the rock. She smiles.

Tuli returns the smile. He is suspicious of the Nun and the Mexican, a very peculiar duo that stands out from his usual clientele.

Tuli looks at the pouch and then at the Nun. "May I?" The Nun nods, confirming authorization. Tuli loosens the ties of the leather bag and empties the contents onto the table. The pink stone tumbles out; Tuli is surprised. He picks up the gem and looks at it; his hand goes under the table. He presses a button. The Nun and the Mexican look at one another. They are getting nervous. They are locked in a series of vaults with no way out. Did they just walk into a scam?

The door to the boardroom opens, and a seventy-year-old man with white hair and glasses enters. He looks like an older version of Tuli. A jeweller's loupe hangs down from a leather strap above his silk tie. The old man comes around the table to stand behind his son. Tuli hands him the stone and says something in rapid Hindi. The old man says nothing. He looks at the Nun and the Mexican. The corners of his mouth move, but it is neither a smile nor a frown. It has the vague appearance of disapproval.

Tuli: "This is my father, Mr. Samkit Dassaani. He is head of the firm." The old man removes his glasses and stuffs them into his breast pocket. He places the jeweller's loupe close to his eye with one hand while rotating the stone with his other. After about thirty seconds, he allows the loupe to drop down on the leather strap. He looks at the Mexican and the Nun. He sniffs or snorts, making a sound that definitely indicates derision. He says something in Hindi to his son. Tuli fires back in rapid Hindi. The old man hands the stone back to his son. "*Nahin!*" He walks out of the boardroom ignoring the Nun and the Mexican.

Nun: "What seems to be the problem?" Tuli raises his hand like a crossing guard at a school crosswalk. He gets up and goes to a credenza that sits back against the wall. He bends over to slide open a wooden panel. He removes a black box and places it on the table beside the stone. Inside the box is a device that determines if a stone is a natural diamond or a man-made imitation.

Mexican: "Do you mind telling us what you're doing with that thing?"

Tuli: "My father says your stone is a fake."

The Mexican slams his hand down on the table. "Bullshit! That stone is real."

Tuli: "Everyone in the business knows the story of the Savola Diamond. A diamond that was presumably stolen and subsequently disappeared. This device should tell us if this is the legendary Savola Diamond."

Nun: "We never said that."

Tuli: "There's not a lot of one-hundred-and-thirty-three carat pink diamonds floating around. This is the Savola Diamond, or it is a fake."

Nun: "So test it." Tuli touches the tip of the tester to the stone.

Tuli shrugs. "This tester only determines thermal conductivity. It can distinguish real diamonds from man-made cubic zirconia, but not stones made from moissanite."

Nun: "So, the test says it's real!"

Tuli: "My father says it isn't." He sits back in his chair. "Where did you get this stone?"

Mexican: "We're not telling you that." The Nun ignores the Mexican. "We got it directly from *Conte* Savola."

Tuli: "Really? Did he give it to you of his own accord or by a more forceful method?"

The Mexican stands up and looks at the Nun. "Come on. Let's get out of here and take the rock to someone who knows what they're talking about."

Nun: "Just wait a damn minute. I want to know if this goddamn thing is real."

Tuli: "Tell me, Sister, are you a real Nun." She starts to object, but he raises his hand. "Let's try one more test." He reaches under the table and presses another button. A middle-aged man in a white coat appears at the door. He enters and hands Tuli another device.

Tuli touches the tip of the tester to the stone; he does it two more times. He hands the tester back to the man in the white lab coat. He says something to the man in Hindi. Who repeats what Tuli just did. The man looks at Tuli and nods. He takes the device and leaves. Tuli puts the pink stone back in the leather pouch and shoves it across the table to the Nun."Your stone is not a genuine diamond. It is moissanite. Most diamond testers can't tell the difference because they only test for thermal properties. But the device I just used tests for electrical conductivity. It says your stone is moissanite, a fake, not the Savola Diamond, but you are certainly free to get a second opinion."

Chapter 20
The *Shicker's* Cane

1970 - College Street, Toronto

Florence carefully makes her way down the stairs from the second-floor lab. The lab manufactures moissanite reproductions of high-value diamonds. Florence recently became aware of the man-made diamond substitute that is difficult to distinguish from the real thing. She learned even most thermal testing devices can't differentiate a genuine diamond from a man-made moissanite stone. The wealthy use the company to create reproductions that can be worn in public while the originals stay safe in a bank vault.

Florence is keenly aware of the inherent dangers of possessing the precious stone hidden in the doll on her desk at home. Her thankfully distant brother, Heinz, was always obsessed with what he called the *Flittchen.* He resented the scar-faced Nun's gift to the five-year-old Florence, and he was near apoplectic when her father stuffed the prized jewel into the doll's innards. As children, Heinz intimidated Florence by attempting to force her to turn over the stone. She refused, "Pappa gave it to me!" she would yell, "Not you!" He vowed to get the stone, no matter how long it took. She understood Heinz would always be a danger to her and her new family, but her brother wasn't the only one who was after the diamond.

Her father promised the gem to the scar-faced Sinarquista Nun in payment for getting the family into Canada. And then there is the current *Contessa* Savola, the rightful owner of the stone. Florence knows possessing the diamond is a risk, but it remains an asset worth holding on to.

Florence clutches her purse close, not wanting to drop it; the moissanite stone it contains may be next to financially worthless, but to her, it has value. It could save her life. Her mind wanders as she approaches the bottom of the staircase. She stumbles, twisting her ankle, as she steps off the last step. She yelps, "God Damn It!"

Her ankle throbs with pain. She opens the door to the street and takes a few steps. She is limping badly. She looks up and down the street for a place to rest. She needs to sit down to give the ankle time to calm down. Across the road, beside the College Street Pawnshop, is the famous Mars Restaurant, where the muffins are *Out Of This World*, at least that is what the neon sign says.

She manages to cross the street to the diner. The place is busy with the lunchtime crowd. Cab drivers, local merchants, and *schmatta* salesmen from the garment district fill the booths and counter stools. One older gentleman notices Florence limping through the door. He drains his last refill of coffee and waves to her to take his seat. She thanks him and takes the brown vinyl-covered stool. She orders coffee and a chocolate chip muffin. When she bites into the muffin, she must concede it tastes *Out Of This World*. Two coffee refills later, she finishes her lunch. She gets up to leave, but her ankle still throbs with pain.

She needs to get to her own restaurant, her husband, George, will be worried, but she can hardly walk. She scans the street for a taxi, but none is in sight. She stands in front of the pawnshop, not knowing what to do. She casually looks in the window, trying not to fall over. She probably shouldn't have had lunch. It only gave her ankle time to swell. She is frustrated and angry at herself for being careless. She notices something of interest in the pawnshop window. She opens the door to the shop and enters.

Sitting in the corner, behind the counter, is an older white-haired man with a neatly trimmed white beard. He wears an open-neck white shirt, unbuttoned dark grey suit vest, and matching suit trousers. He dons a black *yarmulke* and a dour expression. He notices Florence limping badly. His expression softens. He gets up from his seat and approaches her. "Can I help you, young lady?" She recognizes his German accent.

Florence: "Yes, please. That black cane in the window, can you show it to me."

Shopkeeper: "The cane? Are you a *shicker*?

Florence laughs. She knows the expression. "No, sir. I'm not a drunk."

Shopkeeper: "Are you Jewish?"

Florence: "I am what I have to be."

The Shopkeeper nods knowingly. "Aren't we all, young lady, aren't we all." He moves to the window to retrieve the cane. He places it on top of the counter. "It's made of ebony, a gentleman's cane, from another era."

Florence picks up the cane and takes a few steps using the walking stick to keep the pressure off her ankle. "How much?"

Shopkeeper: "This is not a lady's cane, not a lady like you."

Florence smiles: "I don't understand. I hurt my ankle, and I need something to help me get back to work."

The Shopkeeper motions for Florence to give it back to him. He takes the cane from her and unscrews the round knob handle. He holds it up so Florence can see it's hollow. "Not a very good design for a lady's hand." The old man turns the cane slightly, and several glass vials spill out onto the counter. "But an excellent design for a drinker. It's a *Shicker's* Cane."

Florence laughs. "How clever. How very, very clever. I've heard of flask canes, but I've never actually seen one."

Shopkeeper: "I'll find you something else."

Florence: "No, no, it's perfect." She leans over the counter in a conspiratorial manner. She almost whispers. "One can hide more than schnapps in a cane like that."

The Shopkeeper nods. "I understand, my dear, a useful item under certain circumstances." He looks her in the eye. "Are you sure you're not Jewish?"

Florence: "We are both what we have to be. Is that not true, my friend?"

Shopkeeper: "Do you want me to wrap it up for you?"

Florence: "No, I'll need to use it as a cane for the time being."

Chapter 21
Restaurant Renovation

2010 - The Flapper's Club

A young Katrina Klein stands in an empty building that was once her grandparent's downtown eatery. She holds a rolled-up series of blueprints in her hand. Standing with her is her Grandmother, Florence Katrina Dace Klein. It is obvious where Katrina gets her good looks; Florence Klein is a beautiful woman despite her age. At seventy-four, only a few wrinkles, some grey hair, and the necessity of an ebony cane betray her accommodation to age.

Florence: "This is a major renovation, my dear, much fancier than the old place. It will be expensive to renovate."

Katrina: "Yes, I know. I've had the designers draw up preliminary plans. I have an appointment with the bank to see if they'll provide financing."

Florence: "They'll demand collateral, and we already have a mortgage on the building."

Katrina: "The rental income may be enough. We can rent the two upper floors for offices or even apartments. That will help with cash flow. We'll see what they say once they see the plans."

Katrina moves to a work table in the middle of the room. "Come, look at the plans." She unrolls the blueprints and concept sketches onto the table for her Grandmother to see.

Florence looks at the plans carefully. "Very Art Deco; it will be expensive to pull off. What are you going to call it."

Katrina: "The Flapper's Club."

Florence smiles, "Aah, yes, the *Flittchen*, the little doll with a deadly past. We'll need to talk."

Katrina: "Is there a problem?"

Florence: "We'll talk tonight. There are things you need to know. Things I should have told you years ago, things about the *Flittchen*.

Later that evening

Katrina finishes drying the last of the dinner dishes. She is anxious to find out what her Grandmother wants to talk about. Katrina carefully folds the drying towel and hangs it on the handle of the dishwasher. She enters Florence's office; her Grandmother sits at her desk sewing up the back of the *Flittchen*. When she finishes, she looks at the doll with a twinkle in her eye. "There, all better." Also on the desk is a brown leather pouch.

Katrina: "Has the doll been damaged?"

Florence: "Oh, no, not damaged." Katrina is puzzled by her Grandmother's answer. "You see, my dear, the doll is where my Father hid the diamond he stole. It's been hidden in the doll for almost seven decades. I just removed it."

Katrina: "May I ask why? Why now?"

Florence: "Because, my sweet *enkelin*, you may need to use it for collateral. Our new restaurant will be an expensive proposition. We will need to borrow a substantial sum, and we already have a mortgage on the building." Florence removes the sewing kit and places it on the floor. She opens the desk's top drawer and takes out a parchment envelope. She slides the parchment under the brown leather pouch.

Katrina: "Can I see it?"

Florence holds up her hand with one finger raised, signalling Katrina to be patient. She opens her purse and takes out a plain white envelope. She places the envelope beside the parchment one. Florence reaches back into her handbag and removes a second brown leather pouch. She sets it down beside the first one. "Choose."

Katrina instinctively understands what her Grandmother has done. She smiles, "*Oma, du bist eine hinterhältige alte dame.*" Katrina points to the leather pouch on top of the parchment.

Florence opens the leather pouch and removes the diamond. She places it on top of the parchment. Katrina knew the Savola Diamond was unique, an exquisite gem, equal to the most famous and legendary stones in history, but knowing it, and seeing it, are two very different things. Katrina never saw anything like it.

Florence holds up her hand, repeating the gesture for Katrina to be patient. She carefully removes the second diamond from its leather pouch. Florence places it on top of the second envelope. Katrina gets up from her chair to get a better look. "They look the same."

Florence: "Close enough for anyone who is not an expert. Moissanite stones even register as diamonds on most thermal conductivity devices."

Katrina points to the stone sitting on the parchment. "So, that's the real diamond?"

Florence: "Are you sure?"

Katrina: "No. But do you really think your brother, the *Sinarquistas*, or even the current *Contessa* Savola will come after the diamond after all this time?"

Florence: "There are millions of dollars at stake. And yes, I believe that one day, one or all of them will come after us. We must be prepared."

Katrina: "So, which one is the real stone."

Florence: "See for yourself. One envelope holds an invoice for the moissanite stone costing eight hundred and fifty dollars, and the other has a certificate of authentication describing the real diamond in detail."

Katrina picks up the parchment envelope and opens it. She takes out the parchment letterhead inside and reads. It's the invoice for the moissanite stone. She puts the invoice back in the envelope and opens the other envelope. It describes a one-hundred-and-thirty-three carat pink diamond of exquisite quality."

Florence: "You take the diamond and the certificate to the bank. Once we get the loan, put the stone in our safety deposit box. The bank will have its collateral, and we will have our restaurant. Heinz and the others can't get to it as long as it stays in the bank. I'll put the replica in my cane as if I'm hiding it. When they come looking, we have something to give them. By the time they find out it's a fake, we'll be long gone.

Chapter 22
The Red Notice

I know this is a mistake. I've allowed myself to get emotionally involved. And that never ends well for somebody. I've had attractive women as clients before. Some have even found their way into my bed, but none like Katrina. The odds are she is merely using me, but that comes with the territory. The substantial retainer she provided is incentive enough to get in deeper. Perhaps it's just the excuse I need to stay involved. After all, it is what I do for a living. But even if Katrina wasn't paying me, I would still be getting into a taxi at the *Aeropuerto Internacional Benito Juárez*. As long as the Nun and her Nazi associates are on the loose, Katrina, Amadeus, and Charlotte remain in danger. I feel an obligation to all of them.

The Nun and the Mexican must know by now that the diamond they stole is a fake. They've already committed a robbery and a murder; who knows what they'll do next.

The Belgium authorities had Interpol issue a Red Notice for the extradition of Sister Isabella Ramos and Mateo Hernández, the Nun and the Mexican. I finally had official confirmation of their real names. It seems the Belgians don't like people killing foreigners in their hotels. It doesn't do anything to help the tourist trade. But as anticipated, the Mexican authorities, specifically the *Guardia Nacional*, don't seem keen on arresting the pair. It might be due to religious or political sympathy, but more likely a matter of simple corruption. If police corruption was an Olympic event, the Mexicans would definitely be on the podium.

The cab drops me off in front of the Mexico City office of the *Guardia Nacional*. My appointment with Chief Inspector José Diego Martinez is at twelve o'clock. A nice young man in a uniform ushers me into the boardroom, where I am told to wait. Fifteen minutes later, Chief Inspector Martinez enters with a colleague, Subinspector Benito Pérez.

Martinez sits at the head of the table with Pérez off to his right. I take my place at the opposite end. Martinez places a file folder stuffed with papers on the table in front of him. He flips the folder open and shuffles through several forms and notes until he finds what he's looking for. From where I'm sitting, it appears to be the Red Notice. He looks up at Pérez, signalling him to proceed.

Pérez: "Welcome to Mexico, *Señor* Webb. I hope you had a pleasant flight?"

Axel: "Yes, thank you."

Pérez: "You are here about the Red Notice for Sister Isabella Ramos and Mateo Hernández?"

Axel: "Yes, that's correct."

Martinez: "You are a Canadian private investigator, are you not, *Señor* Webb?

Axel: "Yes."

Martinez: "The Interpol Red Notice was requested by the Belgium authorities. I don't see your interest in this matter."

Axel: "Ramos and Hernández robbed one of my clients, *Conte* Savola, while they were in Toronto. I am sure the Mexican authorities don't like foreign nationals being robbed when visiting. Neither do the Canadians. The RCMP were about to request a Red Notice for their extradition to Canada, but the Belgiums had priority since their case is for the murder of Ivars Dace in Antwerp."

Martinez: "Exactly. It seems you have no direct interest in this Red Notice. But even if we were inclined to execute this request, we are not in the habit of arresting Mexican nationals based on scurrilous accusations from obviously prejudiced foreigners looking to blame Mexican tourists for their local crime problems. I'm afraid I can't help you, *Señor* Webb." He flips closed the file folder on the table in front of him. He gets up. "Good Day, *Señor* Webb. Subinspector Pérez will show you out." Martinez leaves the room.

Pérez gets up from his chair and motions to the door. "You have to understand, *Señor* Webb, things are done a little differently here than you are used to." He escorts me to the elevator. He presses the button, and we wait.

Axel: "Bureaucracies everywhere create challenges, but in this case, I don't think Chief Inspector Martinez quite understands the National political implications."

Pérez: "Perhaps we should have a coffee so you can explain."

Chapter 23
A Deal With *El Diablo*

érez and I sit in a café across from the Hotel Geneve. I chose the location because it's where Ramos and Hernández are staying and the place where Otto Dace made his deal with the devil. It hasn't escaped me that the diamond's rightful owners are the *Conte* and *Contessa* Savola, but who knows if the stone still exists in its original form. After so many years, it might be scattered around the globe on the unknowing fingers of a dozen over-pampered brides. I would like to think I'm here to stop a couple of Nazi religious fanatics from turning back the clock eighty-odd years, but perhaps the real reason is Katrina. She has gotten under my skin, and she knows it. The odds are she's using me, but I can't help myself. The Nun and her friend are reason enough to push forward.

Pérez: "So tell me, *Señor* Webb, what national crisis does this Nun and her associate present? I understand this entire situation is about a missing diamond, a large, expensive diamond. Hardly a national emergency."

Axel: "The diamond part is true, but it's the significance of the diamond that you should be concerned with."

Pérez: "I'm afraid you'll have to explain."

Axel: "Ramos and Hernández are part of a group intent on resurrecting an even more extreme version of the Nazi-leaning, Catholic extremist political party, the *Sinarquistas.* The Savola Diamond is how they intend to finance their operation. It's been their goal since the end of WWII."

Pérez: "I am familiar with the *Sinarquistas'* history and their views, but they've long since lost whatever power they had. Mexico has moved on."

Axel: "Has it? Has it really? There is a widespread authoritarian movement, sponsored by Russia and China, giving licence to every crackpot rightwing group to come out from under their rocks and cause disruption."

Pérez: "I'm sorry, *Señor* Webb, but that sounds like one of those crazy conspiracy theories that dominate the Internet. And besides, we have our hands full with the drug cartels and the immigration problem. Nazi hunting is not our business. Best to leave that job to the Israelis."

Axel: "Let's say Ramos and Hernández don't get the diamond. Let's say the diamond no longer even exists. These people will not give up their authoritarian dream; they've been on this same crusade since 1936. They are not going to quit. And if the diamond is unattainable, what do you think they'll do next? If it was you, what would you do?"

Pérez remains silent for a moment. "I suppose they could go after elements in the Church to provide funding and cover."

Axel: "The Church? Maybe, but the Church is Machiavellian. They won't jump in until the group finds a way to fund itself. Sure, they got in bed with Hitler because they saw the handwriting on the wall, but Ramos and Hernández aren't Hitler and Himmler, and the *Sinarquista* isn't the Gestapo. They'll have to establish themselves as a real political force before the Church jumps in. So, tell me? Who has more money than God and is willing to spend it to take over a country and control it politically."

Pérez's eyes go wide. It's like a lightbulb just went off in his head. "The drug cartels!"

Axel: "Exactly. Religion and drugs. A lethal combination. Do you really want an alliance like that running Mexico?"

Pérez goes quiet; he stares at me without saying a word. I stare back. "Are you just going to stand-by and watch it happen? It's not like it has never happened before. Extremist religious groups are sitting in the wings waiting for a worldwide resurrected *La Cristiada* movement."

Pérez: "*Sí*, history has a way of repeating, does it not, *Señor* Webb?"

Axel: "Yes, it does, Benito. It definitely does."

Pérez: "Perhaps there is a way, but one that might not sit well with your Canadian sensibilities. Mexico tends to be ambivalent about how things get done."

Axel: "How much?"

Pérez: "I'm a policeman, Axel; I can't be part of this. I have a career and family to consider, but I have colleagues open to the kind of thing you are suggesting. They will contact you. You can make the arrangement with them."

And so I wait. Two days later, the call comes. I answer. "Axel Webb."

Pérez: "It's me. We have a problem. You may want to cancel."

Axel: "What's the problem?"

Pérez: "My men won't do it unless you go with them. They say it's to identify Ramos and Hernández, but it's if things go sideways, you'll be the one holding the bag. They want five thousand each. You want to back out, say the word."

Axel: "It will take me a day or two to get the cash."

Pérez: "Call me when you've got it, but you better hurry. Who knows when Ramos and Hernández will be on the move? If you want my help, it has to be done here."

As soon as I hang up, I call JoJo and make the arrangement for her and Marco to deliver the cash. If they bring five thousand dollars each, the authorities won't give them any trouble. They're just two tourists looking for a good time while on vacation. This is beginning to be an expensive operation; it's a good thing I'm still on the clock with Katrina. Hopefully, she won't balk at the cost. JoJo and Marco arrive in sunny Mexico the next day. With the cash in hand and JoJo and Marco safely ensconced in an out-of-town resort, I call Pérez to finalize the deal.

The following evening at midnight, I meet two plainclothes *Federales* in the lobby of the Hotel Geneve. They flash a couple of IDs with their index fingers covering their names.

Big Cop: "You have the money?"

I nod, "Yes," and hand each man a folded manila envelope. They check the contents to make sure they contain cash. They don't bother counting. They're not the kind of men you short-change. They stuff the envelopes into their inside jacket pockets. The Small Cop presses 'Six' on the elevator panel. They're not big on conversation.

The elevator stops at the sixth floor; we wind our way through the narrow hallway to Room 617. The Small Cop knocks on the door. Hernández answers. The Small Cop pushes Hernández back into the room; Ramos is on the bed. We enter.

The Big Cop flashes his ID; again with his finger covering his name. "Where is it?"

Hernández: "Where's what?"

Big Cop: "The drugs."

Ramos interrupts. "Can't you see I'm a Nun? We don't have any drugs."

Big Cop: "This is Mexico, Sister; everybody has drugs. Besides, what kind of Nun shares sleeping arrangements with a man?"

Hernández: "Now, just a minute." Hernández notices me standing behind the Big Cop. "What's he doing here?"

Big Cop: "*¡Callate la boca!*"

The Small Cop goes to the dresser and starts pulling open the drawers. Ramos tries to stop him, but he pushes her, knocking her into the bed's footboard. She sprawls onto the carpet. The Small Cop reaches into his pocket and pulls out a packet of white powder. "*¡Lo encontré!*"

Hernández: "That's not ours."

Ramos scrambles to her feet. The Big Cop goes to the television and turns up the volume. He changes channels until he finds an old gangster movie in Spanish with lots of gunfire and shouting. He increases the volume to nine. He nods to the Small Cop, who reaches down, lifts his pant leg, and pulls out a pistol. He approaches where the Nun is standing, turns and fires, hitting Hernández in the middle of his forehead.

Ramos screams.

The Small Cop stands behind Ramos; he puts the pistol to her head and fires. She falls to the floor. He wipes his prints off the gun and places it in Ramos' hand, getting her prints on the handle and trigger. He drops the gun on the carpet beside Ramos.

We leave the hotel room and get in the elevator. Nothing is said until we get to the lobby.

The Big Cop turns to the Small Cop, "Get the lobby and elevator video from security." He turns to me, "You get your money's worth?" I nod.

I expected a drug arrest with extended jail time; what I got for my money was a double murder. I'll admit to being ambivalent about the two dead Nazis, but now that they're dead, Katrina is safe.

Chapter 24
Florence's Floozy

Arrivals, Toronto International Airport

Katrina waits for Aamir al-Uddin, a Bahrainian lawyer from Manama, to clear customs. As he comes through the gate, Katrina sees he is a tall, slim, middle-aged man with well-worn features that look like they should be enshrined in marble. The lawyer wears gold-framed bifocals and a navy British-made bespoke suit. He carries a brown leather briefcase that would cost most people several months' salary. He sports a large, emerald-cut ruby and gold ring, matching cufflinks, a navy and red Italian silk tie, and Gucci loafers. He is a man not afraid to spend money on himself.

After clearing customs, Katrina and al-Uddin exit the airport to a waiting limo that takes the lawyer to the Botsford Arms boutique hotel. The Botsford is owned by a conglomerate rumoured to be controlled by the Bahrainian royal family. As they maneuver through traffic, Katrina and al-Uddin talk. The conversation is casual. The real business will be done in Katrina's office before an anticipated celebratory dinner.

The limo drops al-Uddin at the Botsford before heading to The Flapper's Club. Katrina is excited and a bit sad. The day has already brought both new and lost opportunities.

Several Weeks Earlier

The meeting with Raffy's guy is scheduled for one o'clock at the Dirty Bagel, a Queen Street deli catering to *schmatta* executives in the garment district. The place serves the customary corn-beef, *kishka,* and chicken soup with *knaidlach* cuisine in heart-attack-inducing portions. The conman arrives on time and in character. He is well-dressed. He carries an expensive leather attaché case and speaks with an educated upper-crust British accent. He could easily pass for someone with a Middle Eastern background. I review the details of the plan with him. He shows me the passport and documents he created, identifying him as Aamir al-Uddin, a lawyer for Manama National Trust in Bahrain. They look genuine, authentic enough to convince Katrina that Aamir is the real deal.

Axel: "You'll fly to London tonight; call Katrina and make your pitch. If she's holding the diamond, she'll want to cash it in; it has become a dangerous liability. She is clever and cautious, so make it sound good. Tell her the Prince has a thing for pretty one-of-a-kind trinkets. He owns lots of hotels around the world. He's happy to exchange one minor piece of real estate for the rare pink stone. Make it sound good, but don't lay it on too thick. If she catches any whiff of bullshit, she'll walk."

I hand Aamir his airline ticket and the cash needed for his return flight and hotels. The *Conte* and *Contessa* are funding the operation, despite claiming poverty. I suppose rich people have a different perspective on what constitutes poverty. "The offer is simple the Savola Diamond for the Botsford Hotel. The hotel is valued at roughly fifty million dollars, less than the estimated value of the diamond, but an asset with a substantial cash flow, profit, and a higher potential selling price."

Aamir: "Smart. I understand the diamond has provenance issues."

Axel: "Big time. But this way, Katrina unloads a non-fungible asset at an initial discount, but for a bigger potential legal payout."

Aamir: "Clever. You'd have made a good conman."

Axel ignores the comment. "I actually don't want this to work. I'm hoping she'll tell you she doesn't have the diamond, but you press her hard to see if she cracks. Tell her the Prince's Intelligence people have done their due diligence. They know the diamond she gave the *Conte* and *Contessa* is a fake. Tell her unloading the stone to a conglomerate owned by an unnamed Middle Eastern royal family will guarantee the diamond never reemerges in public. It is the safest, best opportunity she'll ever have to cash in."

Aamir: "If she is as smart as you say, she might smell the con."

Axel: "Maybe, but if she has the stone, she'll want to turn it into something legal."

Aamir: "When she tries to take over the hotel, she'll be shocked she's been taken, but what can she do? The diamond is stolen property."

Axel: "If she's innocent, she won't go for the con."

Aamir: "If she doesn't have the real diamond, who does?"

Axel: "If she doesn't have it. It probably no longer exists, at least not in its original form. Much of its value lies in the legend that goes with it. If it's been cut into several smaller stones, that part of its value is lost. If she has it, she'll go for the deal."

Aamir: "Then what?"

Axel: "You turn the diamond over to me, and I turn it over to its rightful owners, the *Conte* and *Contessa* Savola. They will have it appraised. You and Raffy will split ten percent of my end.

Aamir: "If she has it. I'll get it."

Axel: "One last thing. Don't get any ideas about disappearing with the goods. Raffy and I will have eyes on you the whole time."

Present Day - Before The Airport Pickup

I arrived in Toronto late last night; JoJo and Marco are still in Mexico. They deserve a few days of rest and relaxation. I wait until I get to the office in the morning before calling Katrina.

She is about to leave for the airport to pick up Aamir al-Uddin. Her phone rings. It's Axel. She answers. "You're back."

Axel: "Yes. I came in late last night. I thought we should meet."

Katrina: "Why?" The response is blunt and cold. Maybe she's just tired and busy, but still, it's not the response I expected.

Axel: "You don't have to worry about the Nun and her friend anymore."

Katrina: "Good." Again the answer is stiff and unnecessarily abrupt."

Katrina: "I am rather busy, Axel. I have some important meetings today, and I can't concern myself with these matters. I'm sure you want to get paid, just mail me an invoice, and I'll see it gets looked after immediately. You've been quite useful, and perhaps I can use your professional services again."

My soul, or maybe my heart, is crushed. *'Useful.'* Goddamn it, am I ever stupid. You'd think I've been around long enough to know when I'm being played. I've been dismissed. Whatever thoughts of romance dissipated like the verbal arsenic she just dumped in my morning coffee. I'm a fool. "Okay, sorry to have bothered you. I'll mail the invoice today." I hang up.

Katrina can't figure out why she spoke to Axel that way. She intentionally made him feel like a fool. Was she that afraid of a meaningful relationship? She wanted to see him again. She owed it to him. Whatever he did to the Mexicans cost him, and not just money. The cash she could repay, but gratitude was not in her to give. She knew he had feelings for her; she used them to get what she wanted, plain and simple. She wouldn't dwell on it. She'd move on. It was time to pick up Aamir and finalize the deal, not time for romance.

Business comes first, commerce before pleasure, that is how she lived her life, and it is hard to change. Axel told her the Nun and her associate would no longer bother her. He seemed pretty definitive about that. She could only speculate what that meant.

She could hear the disappointment in his voice, but he said nothing; he just hung up. She's been stupid about the whole thing; she liked Axel, and he was sweet on her; maybe they could reconnect in the future. No, that was wishful thinking. She torched whatever they had between them. The Botsford would have to be compensation enough. She did it, and that was that. Time to move on.

Katrina's Office, Later That Evening

Aamir goes over some last-minute details of the deal with Katrina. Everything goes more smoothly than he anticipated. Katrina is eager to be rid of the diamond. The stone was worth a lot of money, but the Botsford made more long-term business sense. After all, she is in the hospitality business, not the diamond business.

Aamir's eyes are drawn to the framed child's doll with the letter-opener jammed into its chest. "If everything is in order, we can make the exchange tomorrow at the bank, the stone for the deed to the Botsford."

Katrina: "I will be honest with you, Aamir; I am glad to be rid of the thing. There are other beautiful and rare stones, but only a handful have a history like the Savola Diamond."

Aamir: "I can't help but notice the framed doll on your bookcase. It is a rather macabre item, don't you think? You are a beautiful and sophisticated businesswoman, Katrina: so the doll strikes me as an odd trinket to keep. Does it have some special significance?"

Katrina: "The doll, well, yes, it does, funny you should ask." She gets up and hands the framed doll to Aamir. "It's a gift for you."

Aamir smiles: "For me? I don't understand. What am I supposed to do with such a bizarre child's toy? Is it associated with the diamond?"

Katrina: "Let's have dinner, and I'll tell you about Florence's Floozy."

Later The Next Day

The *Conte* Savola rests in a suite at the Yorkville Four Seasons, recovering from the heart attack caused by the violent robbery in the Distillery District. His financial concerns are a thing of the past; his beautiful wife, the *Contessa* Charlotte Dace Savola, sits in my office. She holds the brown leather pouch containing the recovered Savola Diamond. Finally, the Savola legacy has been restored.

Axel smiles at Charlotte. "It is rather ironic, don't you think?"

Contessa: "Ironic? How so?"

Axel: "Not only has the Savola Diamond been returned to its rightful owner, the *Contessa* Savola; it also remains in the hands of the family that stole it."

Contessa: "You know what else is ironic?" Axel shakes his head. "You have a thing for Katrina, and I have a thing for you."

Axel: "Perhaps, that is something we should explore in-depth."

Contessa: "We could start with dinner."

Axel: "At The Flapper's Club?"

Charlotte laughs. "Why not."

The End

Deception

The world is a dangerous place, and every country has men and women tasked to protect it. These people go by many names: secret agent, intelligence officer, and analyst are just a few. Harry is one such person. He is an analyst. He spends his time reading, researching, and analyzing, followed by writing reports that often never see the light of day.

Harry is well educated with a seemingly important job, but Harry is bored. Bored, because analysts never get to be the hero, never get to order cocktails stirred, not shaken, and, never, never, get the girl. Harry is frustrated; frustrated because his superiors told him the report he just spent six months working on is to be tabled, and no, he can't have a field operative to work with to follow up.

Harry has one very dangerous character flaw; he has an imagination, not something the men on the Top Floor appreciate. Harry needs to prove himself. He needs some excitement in his life. And that excitement comes in a deadly package of intrigue and murder that combines something called the *Sister Project* with a Russian master spy, H, K. Kyrsa, code name, the *Beautiful Rat* and the devastatingly gorgeous Harriet. The question is, is it all just happening in Harry's head? Or is there a real plot that needs to be stopped? Is Harry just plain crazy, or are the Russians out to mess with the West one more time? Harry is on his own, not sure who to trust. Are there any good guys in the world of espionage? The only way to find out is to find Kyrsa, the Beautiful Rat. Join Harry in his search for what may not even be real.

DELUSION

Lucy's Breath

Written by Jerry Bader
Illustrated by Paola Ceccant

Delusion: Lucy's Breath

On a chilly November New York City morning in 1953, a scientist working for the CIA on psychotropic mind-control experiments walked off the tenth-floor balcony of the Statler Hotel. He had become increasingly disenchanted with the bizarre and incredibly dangerous work he had been doing in service to national security. Despite the patriotic rationale, the scientist felt his life's work was immoral and most certainly illegal. He wanted out. Unfortunately, he knew too much. And knowing too much is a very precarious position to be in, if you work for a clandestine operation run by America's very own version of Josef Mengele, the Angel of Death.

The scientist insisted on getting out, and out he got, through the window and off the balcony of the Statler Hotel on that brisk Fall morning in Manhattan. Was suicide his solution for terminating his deal with the devil, or did the devil do him in? It's impossible to say. The evidence, although in plain sight is murky and blurred by time and the self-preservation of those responsible. I know what you're thinking, not in my America, not in my beloved United States, not in the home of the brave and the land of the free. Unfortunately, it did happen; it's the kind of thing that happens when governments feel an existential threat.

America has a fundamental flaw, an Achilles heel of perspective and attitude; it fails to understand history and its place in it. In the words of philosopher, George Santayana, "Those who cannot remember the past are condemned to repeat it." If you believe it can't happen here, I urge you to look at The Wall Street Putsch of 1933 and the name of one of the participants. You might find it informative. It could happen again. America is under siege by a series of existential threats. It's not some crackpot conspiracy theory; it's history. The question I have is: which is more dangerous, the external threat or the internal threat?

For those who cling to Senator Barry Goldwater's Cold War aphorism, "Extremism in defence of liberty is no vice." I urge you to remember the past because if you don't, you will be condemned to a future you did not expect and an existence you will be forced to endure. What follows could happen, and maybe will happen if you allow extremism to take hold of the levers of power.

Dilemma: Mozart's Medicine

A poisoned accountant, a Chinese painter with an infamous Italian name, the People's Minister of Science and Technology, his brother the Director of the Enterprise Division of the Ministry of State Security, and Harry, the art dealer who moonlights as a Secret Intelligence Service agent are the players in the search for why D. D. Greyson was poisoned by a seventeenth-century Italian cosmetic favoured by disillusioned wives. The business of intelligence is a simple proposition: gather enough data so the politicians can make informed, rational decisions on things like national security or on whether or not one of the several competing forces in the world is about to go all ballistic on your ass.

The problem is not too little information but too much. There are cameras everywhere and facial recognition software that allows agencies to track anyone's movement day and night. The various intelligence services have so much information, it becomes difficult to decide what is relevant, actionable, or even real. It is the paradox of choice, the paralysis of analysis, or if you prefer, the spy's dilemma. No one knows what is real, what is noise, or what is purposeful misdirection.

And so, our hero, Harry, becomes a player, not because he is particularly brave or expert in the art of manipulation or even killing, but rather because he has an imagination. He is a man who can conjure reality out of abstraction. And that particular skill can be a very important asset when it comes to playing three-player Chinese checkers with competing Beijing interests.

The worlds of art and national security collide on the streets of London, leaving a trail of burned paintings, payoffs, dead bodies, and deadly microchips.

Diversion: Ahab's Folly
A Tale of Spies, Lies, and Wise-Guys

Harry is drawn back into the Quandary orbit when his restaurant partner goes missing, and a dead North Korean RGB agent is found murdered on Benten Island under the torii gate of the Itsukushima Shrine, near Matsumae Castle in Hokkaido, Japan. A Japanese Naicho CIRO Agent, a Mossad, Kidon Agent, and twin brother casino operators join Harry and his Quandary colleagues to unravel the latest attempt by the Chinese and North Koreans to disrupt the financial institutions in the West.

Are the documents found on the dead RGB agent clues to a North Korean kidnapping scheme to raise money to pay their Chinese benefactors for keeping the Kim regime afloat? Or, perhaps, the purpose is merely to keep the North Korean Generals well-stocked in the finest Irish whiskey and French Champagne so the Supreme Leader can sleep with at least one eye closed? On the other hand, maybe it's a smokescreen, a feint attack to hide the real, more nasty and nefarious plot to cause havoc in the situation rooms of Whitehall and the White House. And what does Harry's missing business partner have to do with it? Is the missing Sydney Katz just a coincidence? But then, Harry doesn't believe in coincidences.

Defection: Dragonfly
Three Women, Three Agendas, One Dragonfly

Defection, details the kidnapping of Rita Daveed, aka Harriet. The MSS needs to retrieve an audio SD card that will reveal the identity of Dragonfly, a Chinese sleeper agent embedded high-up in Vauxhall Cross. *Defection* is a story of treason, betrayal, and revenge. Three women with varying agendas clash over identifying the elusive spy known only as Dragonfly.

Before Rita is taken on orders from Yang Bo, the Director of the UFWD, she manages to leave behind a clue, a postcard from the Bowley Gallery in London, with a cryptic message scrawled on the back, "Find Harry!"

Yang Hu, an MSS agent and daughter of Yang Bo, decides she's had enough international intrigue. She makes the decision to defect to Great Britain. Hu's get-out-of-China-alive card is her knowledge of who Dragonfly really is.

She contacts Arty Pearl, Rita's boyfriend, telling him she knows where Rita is being held. In return, she wants Arty to inform Harry: MI6 has a mole. The Quandary Team, now led by Harry, finds circumstantial evidence to suggest Alice May, the Special Assistant to the Chief of SIS, is Dragonfly. Sir William refuses to believe his longtime assistant is a spy. But he does authorize Harry to arrange Yang Hu's defection on the condition she reveals the true identity of the mole. Unfortunately, Sir William dies of a heart attack before Harry can make the arrangements. The new Acting Chief is a former Cabinet Minister and party hack, Thomas Burgundy-Smith. Burgundy-Smith rescinds the defection order, fires Harry, disbands Quandary, and promotes Alice May.

Rita escapes and begins to plot her revenge; Yang Hu puts her Plan B into action, and Alice May continues to disrupt the MI6 operations from her position of influence. Three women, three agendas, and one spy connive, maneuver, and manipulate the intelligence landscape for advantage, security, and revenge.

The Outlaw Rider
"If you're not prepared to cheat,
you're not prepared to win."

Jesse James, the daughter of a deceased mob-connected rug salesman, becomes a jockey working for the *Hong Mian* triad in order to feed winners to State Senator Samuel Somersby. The Senator is responsible for approving California gaming licenses. To date, only Native CANGV casinos are allowed to have slots. California horse racing will die if they aren't allowed to add slot machines to their venues. Benson Yeung, Dragon Head of the *Hong Mian* triad, and his chief lieutenant, Johnny Luck, have a plan to force Somersby to approve their Native partner's demands for off-reservation gaming licenses. At the center of the plan is a unique white thoroughbred Spirit horse, prized by Native people, appropriately named Medicine Hat.

Dead End
There Are No Good Guys

It all started five years earlier with the murder of Peter Pretty Boy Chen, a low-level soldier for Benson Yeung's Hong Mian triad. Rumor had it that the Guan Yu statue that sat on the old man's desk, the symbol of his Dragon Head status as leader of the Hong Mian, was filled with priceless Pigeon Blood rubies, or at least that's what Peter Pretty Boy Chen thought. Whether he was right or wrong is a tale for another time and another place.

What's significant is his desire to get his hands on those rubies led to his brains being splattered all over the wall of the Green Dragon Restaurant. Like all classic California mysteries, the past is never forgotten or forgiven; it always comes back to raise its ugly head.

Fast forward five years. We first met Jesse James and her associates in *The Outlaw Rider* when she was a young female jockey making a name for herself on the track and off under the guidance of her mentor, triad big shot, Johnny Luck. Jesse has moved up the Hong Mian ladder and has made herself a senior triad player, but the past is never so far behind that it doesn't affect the present. And so *Dead End* begins.

Palermo
A Place To Die

The race took place in picturesque Palermo, Sicily, but this wasn't your typical horse race with rules designed to protect the horses, jockeys, and bettors. This was a Mafia-sponsored street race: a blood sport free-for-all more suited for the Coliseum than the backstreets of the scenic Sicilian town. Race promoter Santos Luzzato, nephew to Nicky The Mushroom Fungo, wanted in on his American Uncle's horse racing connections with the LA triads. The race leads to a series of decisions that end with a suspicious car accident that kills billionaire heiress and racehorse owner Josephine Somersby Murphy, sister to Governor Samuel Somersby, a man with Presidential ambitions and ties to Johnny Luck, LA triad big shot.

Love, sex, murder, and racehorses create a toxic mix of intrigue and suspense that drives Luck's protégé, Jesse James, to Sicily, Argentina, England, and Switzerland in her pursuit of the truth. Who killed Josephine Murphy? Was it Luzzato, Nicky Fungo, Murphy's brother, the Governor, or someone closer to Jesse? Palermo, a place to die.

Stone Cold
Between a Stone and a Hard Place

On the surface, Major William Stone (Retired) is merely a wealthy English expatriate with a diverse military and financial services background now living in Palermo, Argentina, where he runs a small art gallery with his assistant Margarita Cervantes.

If you scratch the surface, you'll find that Stone was recently the chauffeur for Mrs. Josephine Murphy, heiress to the Murphy Peanut Butter Company, the largest peanut butter manufacturer in the USA, and owner of numerous expensive thoroughbred racehorses. This odd set of circumstances gets even more intriguing when you learn that Stone inherited over one billion dollars when Murphy died in a questionable car accident in the hills of Palermo, Sicily. After the Murphy estate is settled, Stone disappears to reemerge in Argentina, leading a quiet and peaceful life as a wealthy art gallery owner and financier. His good fortune is tempered because he left Jesse James, protégé to gangster Johnny Luck, back in LA.

The problem is Major William Stone died in the Falkland Islands and the man now assuming his modified identity is disgraced MI6 financial wizard Jacob Conrad. Conrad took the fall for his Vauxhall Cross masters' illegal shenanigans, ending in jail with a lengthy prison term. According to the British newspaper reports, Conrad died in Belmarsh Prison, only to be resurrected by Section Six's cyber boffins as William Stone, international financial consultant living in Hong Kong. In Hong Kong, Stone runs into Charlie Long, Dragon Head of the Wan Chai and a rival of the Hong Mian, led by Benson Yeung and Johnny Luck.

Stone Cold dives deep into the back story of how Jacob Conrad becomes William Stone, why he disappeared, leaving Jesse behind, and who'll control the flow of cocaine into the USA. From Hong Kong to Palermo, London, Cacaloxuchitl, Mexico and Los Angeles, this is a tale of secret agents, drug dealers, money launders, and murders, all wrapped in a delicious recipe of greed, envy, cocaine, and peanut butter chilli.

The Aussie Switch
Published By MRPwebmedia

Horse trainers Davey and Pauly Cisco are looking for a fresh start in Southern California after wearing out their welcome in their native Australia. The Cisco twins are identical in looks but not personality; Pauly, like most horse trainers, pushes the envelope of acceptable practice while his look-alike brother rips through regulations with regularity and abandon. It didn't take long for the two brothers to hook up with a couple of conmen: an expert computer hacker who likes e-gaming and a shyster stock promoter on the lookout for eager marks willing to blow their fortunes on a shady horse-betting consortium. The one thing they didn't count on is an associate of Benson Yeung's Hong Mian triad, an ex-South Korean Colonel who operates a shady international gambling empire. Two corrupt confidence men, unethical twin horse trainers, and doppelgänger thoroughbreds add up to a combustible confluence of confusion, misdirection, and murder, with tentacles that twist their way through LA, Sidney, Hong Kong, Seoul, and Macao.

Ballet of Bullets
The Game Is Dodging Death
Published By MRPwebmedia

Internet gambling and the expansion of casinos beyond the Nevada State Line have put a financial strain on racetracks. Johnny Luck, Hong Mian triad big shot, and his beautiful blonde ex-jockey protege, Jesse James, are always looking for ways to expand the triad's gambling operation. In the fifties and sixties, Jai Alai was a big deal in Florida. Gamblers would fill the *frontons* and drop thousands of dollars betting on Basque athletics competing in a sport that was so dangerous it was referred to as the Ballet of Bullets and, The Game Is Dodging Death.

Johnny Luck sees the potential revenue that could be produced by resurrecting the all but dead blood sport. The question is, how to make it popular again? Jesse has the answer. Television. People will bet on anything; they will also watch anything, as witnessed by the plethora of cooking shows that feature ordinary people competing for who can fry the best egg.

If there's a competition, people will bet on who will win. But where there is money, there is corruption; enter the Miami Bettor's Club, run by old Hong Mian rivals Tommy The King Kong and Marco Antonia Suarez, nicknamed *El Astronauta*. In the end, the Ballet of Bullets becomes all too real for the people fighting for control of the gambling revenue generated by the International Jai Alai League.

www.ingramcontent.com/pod-product-compliance
Lightning Source LLC
Chambersburg PA
CBHW051245170626
46809CB00004B/1502